PENNY OATES

◆

LOVE CHILD

Complete and Unabridged

LINFORD
Leicester

First published in Great Britain in 2019

First Linford Edition
published 2020

A catalogue record for this book is available
from the British Library.

ISBN 978–1–4448–4582–2

Published by
Ulverscroft Limited
Anstey, Leicestershire

Set by Words & Graphics Ltd.
Anstey, Leicestershire
Printed and bound in Great Britain by
T. J. International Ltd., Padstow, Cornwall

This book is printed on acid-free paper

Prologue

She couldn't believe they had gone — left without a word! She remembered all the promises he'd made her, about how she would always be able to see Lara, watch her growing up and know she was safe and loved. Once she had hoped to persuade him that they could admit their transgression and acknowledge their child, but he had been horrified at the thought of the scandal, and she'd eventually realised that the only fair outcome was to agree to the adoption.

He had been surprised — she'd been so adamant in her refusal to give up the baby initially, and it had taken all his charm and powers of persuasion to get her to sign the fostering papers.

He pretended to regret their action, but she knew that secretly he had been pleased. Standing was so much more

1

important to him than understanding, she thought, and with a sudden flash of insight she recognised that he must have been party to this midnight flit.

Their daughter's adoptive parents had been his employees, for heaven's sake, and were still pretty feudal in their allegiances. They never would have departed without his blessing. In fact, she doubted they would have left at all unless he had planted the idea in their minds.

She stared through the car windscreen at the little tied cottage, her view blurred in spite of the efficient wipers smacking smartly from side to side. She realised it was her tears that were blinding her, and wiped them with the backs of her hands, but her improved sight simply made her feel more wretched — now she could see clearly the curtain-less windows and empty rooms. Small, cramped rooms that he had avoided but that she had insisted on visiting. Rooms where she had found the warmth and welcome of the farm worker and his wife a balm to her tangled feelings; feelings which proved she had found the love of her life, yet also acknowledged that love did not mean perfection.

When she saw her baby in another woman's arms it was hard to bear, but at least she liked and admired the woman, and knew she would always be welcome in her home.

Or she had thought she would be. Now, in front of the cold, empty house, she knew she would never see the little family again.

It was his work — it had to be his work — his job always came first, and that depended on the social niceties. No illegitimate children here, thank you, only those born in wedlock were acceptable.

A wave of despair swept over her and made her feel sick. It had nothing to do with her hormonal condition; it was bile, the bitter taste of remorse and blame. It rose unbidden, together with the start of the canker that would drive them apart.

He would never acknowledge their baby. Lara was lost to them both.

'*I have given suck and know how tender 'tis to love the babe that milks me.*' She was hardy aware she spoke, but the great emptiness inside her echoed Lady Macbeth's words.

She thought her heart would break.

1

'You're certainly sitting pretty now you've inherited this house.' Malcolm looked around the kitchen with his mean little eyes, and Lara had to stifle the desire to throw the contents of the pan in front of her all over him. 'Yes, you fell on your feet when Uncle Dan and Aunty Jennifer adopted you.'

She counted to ten under her breath. She had known it was going to be a difficult day from the moment she had woken up and remembered that Malcolm was coming for lunch. That meant she hadn't been able to have her normal Saturday morning lie in, but had to drag herself downstairs to prepare for her visitor.

The little terraced house seemed cold and empty without Mum and Dad, and she'd turned the television on low simply to have some background sound as she busied herself.

She hadn't been looking forward to Malcolm's visit, and had put him off for as long as she could, but eventually she'd had to agree a date. He was her dad's nephew and had always taken a proprietary interest in both her and her possessions, from her toys in their childhood to her inheritance now.

As a child he had given her the creeps, but he'd improved a little with age, although she still resented his assumption that she was his for the taking. She'd had to suffer Mum's match-making machinations, too — Mrs Dunstan had thought it would be wonderfully romantic if the adoptive cousins married each other some day, but her dad had been a lot more understanding.

'He's not for you, princess,' he'd said. 'Oh, I know your mum thinks it would be a good idea because you've known each other all your lives, but you and I know that familiarity breeds contempt! And I grew up with his mother, don't forget, and Aunty Pat had the same domineering attitude as her son. What Malcolm wants is a quiet, obedient wife, and I don't see you fitting the bill, do you?'

They'd chuckled together and avoided mentioning the other reason that Mrs Dunstan hoped for an inter-family marriage . . .

She and her husband had almost given up hope of having a baby before Lara arrived. They had married late and by the time they realised they would need to adopt children rather than have their own, their ages were against them. So it had seemed like a fairytale come true when Mr Dunstan had been approached by his boss and asked if he would be prepared to foster a baby girl whose mother was unable to keep her.

The woman from social services hadn't been pleased about the irregular way the arrangement had first been made, but Mrs Dunstan had been determined to win her over, and eventually, when the birth mother decided to put Lara up for adoption, she had supported the Dunstans' application to become her legal parents.

'The day you became ours was the happiest of our life.'

How often Mum had said those words, and it was clear they were nothing but the truth. She was less forthcoming about why the little family had then moved away. But without being told, Lara understood it was to save any embarrassment with her natural mother still living in the area.

'We loved you so much!' her mum would say.

Lara knew this was also nothing but the truth, and as she grew she recognised that so too did her mother's love — along with her anxiety.

Devoted to her daughter, Mrs Dunstan was always just a little afraid that she might lose her like some beautiful changeling; that when the child grew to be a woman, she would fly the nest and return to her own kind. So marrying Malcolm would bind her to the

Dunstans and ensure her place among them forever.

'Oh, Mum, I never would have left you,' Lara said aloud now as she tidied up. 'No one ever could have taken your place.'

To take her mind off her sadness, she turned her attention to the flickering television screen. It was a current affairs programme, not guaranteed to cheer anyone up, she decided, and was about to change channels, when a man on screen caught her attention.

The item was about Hal Lawrence, the elder statesman whom all the papers were predicting would be nominated for an important position to support the labyrinthine European negotiations during this difficult time. The camera had panned back from the politician's face to include his younger companion. He was, thought Lara, exceptionally good looking, but there was something more — a well controlled authority coupled with the air of a man it would be foolish to cross

9

— she found it hard to articulate exactly. But whatever it was it was certainly potent — and there was no doubt he had taken her mind off her own problems!

At that moment, a hooded young man raced towards the politician, arm poised ready to throw what looked like an egg at him, and in a flash the object of Lara's pleasant daydreams leapt into action. The politician's minder disarmed the activist and dispatched him out of camera range.

It was the release she had needed. Talk about basic instinct — she had been panting over a politician's minder! *Still, he could take care of me any time,* she thought, which surprised her, as she was usually very self-sufficient.

Mum had constantly drummed into her that women needed to be the strong ones in any relationship, because they always carried the can if anything went wrong. Lara knew that Mrs Dunstan had been trying to protect her from the fate of her birth mother, and she had taken the message on board: break the rules and the consequences can be tragic.

They weren't tragic for me, though, Lara thought. Although it had made her determined never to end up in the same situation. Indeed, Mrs Dunstan's frequent refrain had been about how 'nice girls didn't'.

She was secure in her parents' love. She had always known she was adopted, and even though as she became older and more curious their answers to her questions about her early life had not fully satisfied her, she never doubted their absolute commitment to her.

Malcolm arrived promptly at twelve, and Lara was pleased to discover he was more subdued than usual. An uneasy truce had developed between them following their last meeting, when he had called her a 'frigid feminist' for telling him that she was her own woman, that the house she had inherited was hers, and that she had no intention of living with him, then or ever.

For a while afterwards he had given her the space she desired, but a few weeks earlier he had recommenced his regular phone calls, and when she had finally run out of excuses to keep him at arm's length, she had reluctantly invited him to lunch.

'The garden's looking a bit overgrown,' he said as she stirred the food in the wok. 'You need a man to cut the hedge.'

'No, I don't.' She smiled, too sweetly. 'I can do it myself.'

'I could mow your lawn.'

'I like it long, it encourages wildlife.'

She hoped she wouldn't have to slap him down all afternoon and was relieved when he behaved quite well. He didn't make a pass at her as he often did, and seemed eager to please.

Too eager.

'Lara, have you ever thought of trying to contact your real parents?' he asked as they drank their coffee after the meal.

12

'No, I've never really felt the need. Mum and Dad were all I wanted.'

'While they were alive, yes, but what about now you're alone?'

She shook her head. 'I'm too raw. They've only been gone six months . . .' It seemed only yesterday they had been here beside her.

'The paper is doing a feature on adult children searching for their roots, and I immediately thought of you.'

Typical! Lara pulled a face. Malcolm was an up and coming reporter on the local free newspaper, always on the look out for the big story that would help him make the leap to one of the nationals. She thought he had the temperament for it — pushy and careless of the feelings of others.

'It's just my mother always said there was something funny about your adoption,' Malcolm continued, indifferent to the body language that might have told a more sensitive man to stop. 'Uncle Dan was over fifty when he and Aunty Jen got you, way past the age

13

most adoption agencies will consider. And then there was the fact that he moved away from Wyscom and came to London. Why would your real family have wanted you gone? Once you were adopted, what would it have mattered where you lived? Mum said that your dad always hated towns, yet he gave up a life he loved to come and work with Dad at Bentars and live here.' He looked around the small dining room dismissively.

While her parents had been quite open with her, Lara was aware they had been less forthcoming about her background to others, particularly to Dan Dunstan's overbearing sister. Her father had worked on a farm in Surrey, and Lara believed it was the owner of the farm who had made all the arrangements for her adoption. She had assumed it was the daughter of the house who had been her birth mother, and that the family were not prepared to support the girl in keeping the baby.

Like many adopted children, she had

fantasised about being a true love child, but it did not cause her any distress. She was sure that no blood tie could be closer than the bonds that tied her to the Dunstans, and recognising her mother's insecurity, she made no attempt to find out about her early past while Mrs Dunstan was alive.

She'd even gone out with Malcolm on a number of occasions to make Mum happy. A foolish decision, she later recognised, as it encouraged his feelings of ownership, and she'd had to make it clear that she was not ready to settle down with anyone, let alone him.

The trouble was, whereas she had felt safe in her decision when her parents were alive, after they died within six months of each other, she missed her dad's strong support.

Malcolm had tried to assume a role his position as cousin didn't warrant, issuing instructions and making plans on her behalf, and it had taken all her spirit to stand up to him in her bereaved state. But when he had glibly assumed he would move into her parents' house without an invitation they had fallen out, and then he had accused her of leading him on.

She knew she hadn't encouraged him, so ignored the implication that she had, but the frigid bit gave her pause for thought.

There had been boyfriends, of course, and she was not falsely modest and knew men found her attractive. On one level she had been flattered by the interest they showed and welcomed the companionship. However, whenever her partners moved towards a closer relationship, she backed away quickly. It wasn't that she didn't enjoy closeness but the moment it seemed that things were getting serious, she would step away.

Did that mean she was cold? She didn't know. All she knew was that it didn't feel right, and she was going to trust her instincts.

'There was nothing strange about my

adoption.' Lara set her mouth firmly. 'You've been reading so many of those silly season stories in the newspapers that you're beginning to believe anything.'

She pinched her lips tightly together. Now they were dead, she didn't intend to answer the prying questions of Aunty Pat's son. She knew Dad had loved the countryside but hadn't realised what a wrench leaving the farm to ensure a new start for his baby had been. Houses were expensive in London, and it had meant he'd had to work well past retirement age to provide for his family. He'd still been part-time at Bentars when he died.

Absurdly she felt guilty, and then annoyed with Malcolm for giving her the information that made her feel that way.

'Dad told me the work on the farm was getting too heavy, and he found working at Bentars much easier. That's why he moved here — nothing mysterious about it at all — there isn't much alternative employment in the country.'

Malcolm managed to look triumphant and sly at the same time.

'Well I intend to find out,' he said, 'even if you don't want to be in the article. I'm going to see what I can discover about your mysterious past.'

'How dare you interfere in my life like this!' Lara was enraged. 'Whoever my birth parents are, it's absolutely nothing to do with you.'

'Yes it is. Uncle Dan and Mum were brother and sister, and — '

'And as you have been at pains to make clear, were absolutely no blood relation to me! I was the one who was adopted — not Dan, not Aunty Pat, not you — and *I'll* decide whether I want my background looked into, not you!'

Malcolm glared back at her.

She could see he was angry that she wasn't reacting as he had imagined she would. No doubt he'd expected her to throw her arms around him and thank him for doing this for her!

Plainly he had assumed that most adopted children wanted to know where they came from, and she was pretty sure he had seen her as his entree into what looked like being an important featured article. She knew he was ambitious and only ever saw things from his point of view, so because he longed to see his name in print in a national paper, he assumed she would want that too, or would at least be prepared to help him get there.

'You've been incredibly mean since your parents died!' he stormed. 'You inherited this house which would make a great pad for us both, being so near my work, yet you won't even let me move in!'

Lara didn't respond. She was well aware Malcolm wanted to get out of the flat he shared with three other undomesticated men — and not only because she was neat and organised and could cook and he saw her doing all those tedious chores for him.

She recognised that she had the type

of looks — rounded curves and fair hair — that some men would see as an asset to be flaunted in front of their friends, and she knew that was all Malcolm wanted. She wasn't really his type — he liked his women small and adoring — but he would not be averse to having a trophy blonde on his arm if only just for show.

'Your mother would have wanted you to help me,' he shouted, 'I'm just glad she isn't here to see how selfish you're being!'

It was too much for Lara.

'Get out, get out!' she yelled, leaping to her feet and pulling on his arm.

'With pleasure!'

He stormed towards the door.

'You're a spoilt brat! My mother always said Aunty Jennifer acted as if you were better than the rest of us. Well you're not, Lara! The only thing that makes you different is that your real mother didn't have the sense to use birth control!'

He slammed the door as he left, and

Lara found herself crying hot tears of rage which melted into shuddering sobs of loss.

Was she selfish? Had she been spoilt? It was true her parents had doted on her and had given her lots of attention, but they had also taught her to value others and to be kind.

Deep inside, Lara knew Malcolm had lashed out to hurt her with his words because she wouldn't do what he wanted, but she still worried it was her fault that her father had left his beloved countryside.

As her misery subsided, she noticed Malcolm had left behind the notebook he carried at all times and into which he scribbled down his journalistic leads. She stretched out her hand to read it. Would it have anything about her?

She found her name, but it was on a page of indecipherable jottings that made little sense to her. There was an incomplete family tree — no father was shown, which she had expected, but in the box for 'mother' he had written

'Chloe' followed by a question mark.

The door bell interrupted her reverie. Malcolm back for his notebook she didn't doubt. Well, she wasn't going to give it to him.

She strode to the front door and put the chain on the lock before opening the door just enough to speak her message.

'I'm not letting you back in to discuss birth control again!' She knew her voice sounded shrill, but she was still very angry with him.

'Well that's a relief,' a well modulated baritone replied. 'I find that it's generally never a good conversation opener.'

Lara's eyes widened in embarrassed surprise. Oh hell! Why hadn't she looked out through the spy hole before opening the door?

Now she would just have to brazen it out with whoever was outside. She peered round the door frame to see who her mystery caller was — and felt her mouth drop open into a large, round '0' like that of a fish.

Standing on her doorstep was Hal Lawrence's minder, resplendent in suit and tie in spite of it being the weekend.

He was drop dead gorgeous, incredibly sexy — and laughing at her discomfiture!

2

'What do you want?' She sounded pretty ungracious, Dominic thought, but maybe she was just being wary. 'I already belong to Neighbourhood Watch, you know, to keep away undesirables,' she went on.

'Oh, I can do desirable.' He gave an easy smile. 'My name is Dominic Leigh and I work — '

'For Hal Lawrence, I know,' Lara interrupted.

So she knew about the Lawrences. He had expected it but was disappointed nevertheless.

He'd had some difficulty tracing her, and when he'd finally managed to get a photo of her he'd been struck by the ethereal beauty of the girl now before him. Personal experience had left him with a jaded view of women, yet in spite of that, it seemed to him that the quality her picture had radiated most was innocence.

However, her response to him now proved what life had taught him — women were not to be trusted and were out for what they could get.

'May I come in?'

'Why?' She sounded belligerent.

'I want to talk to you about your parents.'

'They're dead.' She said it with a flat finality, but he saw the pain in her face.

'I heard about the Dunstans.' His tone was sympathetic. 'But actually I wanted to talk about your birth parents.'

She'd looked over his shoulder as he spoke, as if unwilling to meet his gaze, but his words brought her eyes back to his. Expressive, green pools that gave away her thoughts. He watched as she struggled between interest and puzzlement.

Finally she made her decision. 'Come in.'

'What do you want?' she asked when

they were settled in a small, neat sitting-room. 'Why are you interested in my birth parents?'

He shrugged. 'I wondered if you knew who they were, that's all.'

'So you came all the way here to ask me? You'll have to do better than that.'

She was no fool, and he didn't blame her for being suspicious — it *was* suspicious! What on earth was he doing here?

'Hal Lawrence knew the Dunstans,' he said quietly. 'And he wondered if they'd ever spoken to you about your natural parents.'

'Mum didn't like talking about my adoption.' Lara looked at a framed family photo on the mantelpiece. 'She was afraid of losing me.'

'I can understand that.'

Anyone lucky enough to have the girl sitting opposite would want to keep her close.

'Look, what has this got to do with Hal Lawrence? Frankly, what Mum talked to me about is none of his business.'

'The Dunstans used to work on his estate many years ago and Hal only recently heard about their deaths. He just wanted to be sure you were OK. He's always been very concerned for his staff.'

Well, that bit at least was true — Hal did have a loyalty to old retainers. It was why his employees rarely left him. Dominic didn't like lying and knew he was stretching the truth, because the real reason he was here was to make sure that Lara wasn't an unbalanced virago who would cause Hal trouble.

'In Surrey? No, my father used to work on a farm in a place called Wyscom.'

She eyed him warily and Dominic felt she was fencing with him. Was she being disingenuous, or did she really not know? He feared he was being enchanted by her lovely face, but he mustn't let himself be fooled by her appearance.

'So I understand. Did he ever say who your real parents were?'

'The Dunstans were my real parents,' she said firmly, 'and no, I know nothing about my birth parents. Why would I be interested in people who didn't want me?'

She had a point, why would she? He only hoped she didn't see her adoption as abandonment which needed retribution, but he was pleased to see she was pretty level-headed.

He sighed. He hadn't wanted to come prying, but Hal had been tense and worried about his position, so Dominic had agreed to find out whether any ghastly secrets were likely to be let out of the bag before the selection committee met. He was glad Lara seemed unaware and disinterested in her past. It made his job easier and allowed him to think of her as a beautiful woman rather than a tool for the opposition who needed to be controlled.

He did indeed find her beautiful. The fundamental response he'd felt when she opened the door and he looked into her clear green eyes proved the attraction. Usually he held back, having learned the hard way that involvement meant pain, but today his thoughts seemed to be going in another direction.

The ringing of a phone pulled his thoughts back on track and she left the room to find her mobile.

He idly picked up a notebook from where it had fallen open on the floor. As he did so his eye caught the name 'Chloe' in the family tree, and he needed to go no further.

He put the notebook on the table — he had the answer he had been seeking.

So she was a liar as well as a beauty.

He was surprised by the stab of disappointment which quickly turned to anger at himself for being taken in by outward show. He knew women, knew the little games they played. Why had he hoped this one would be any different?

'I thought you didn't know anything about your natural parents,' he said when she re-entered the room.

'I don't, but you can tell me about them, can't you?' She didn't seem to have picked up on his accusation. 'Hal Lawrence must have said something to you.'

Her denial made him even angrier, but he did his best to hide his true feelings.

'Not really. He just wanted to know you were all right, and now that I've ascertained you are, I must go.'

He stood up. He mustn't give the game away. She might already know the truth, but he had to act as if nothing untoward had happened. At least she only had the first name, but he needed to warn Hal that all hell could break lose if the opposition found out about his Achilles heel.

★   ★   ★

Lara tried not to show her disappointment as he rose to leave, her dissatisfaction not solely due to the fact that he couldn't tell her about her birth mother.

She let him out of the front door and then returned to the notebook, but her thoughts wandered elsewhere. She had been unsettled by her visitor, with his self-confidence and slightly superior manner. He had given her the impression he was humouring her — playing some game that she was not a party to. Their interview had not been a comfortable one, yet part of her had enjoyed it and was disappointed she wouldn't be seeing him again. What was all that about?

He was attractive, of course, but character always meant more to her than good looks, so her response was all the more surprising. She had to admit, Dominic Leigh had awakened her interest, and she had the strangest feeling that there was more to his visit than met the eye. His probing had intrigued her and if he wouldn't tell her what it was all about, well then, she would just have to find out for herself.

That this might allow her to see him again she pushed to the back of her mind, unwilling to examine her feelings.

However, she did acknowledge that concerning her birth parents there could be no turning back. She had told Malcolm it would be her decision whether or not to seek them out. Now, with her imagination fired by the minder's visit, she was determined to do so. But where to start looking?

* * *

'Try social services.' Her best friend, Michelle suggested. They'd met on the first day of junior school and been friends ever since. She made this suggestion when Lara phoned her to tell her about the strange visitor — though she refrained from saying anything about how his presence had unsettled her. Some information was too embarrassing even for best friends.

She'd told Michelle she would do just that, but when she approached the local social service department for the Wyscom area, they informed her that all their adoption records had been lost in a warehouse fire, and that unfortunately, her adoption had taken place before personal information was stored electronically.

It seemed she was beaten at the first hurdle.

'I wonder how Malcolm came up with the name Chloe, and whether it's correct. I suppose you could phone and ask him.'

It was a Saturday, and Michelle had popped round on her way to work. She was a nurse at the local hospital and as her route passed right in front of the Dunstan home, she often popped in for a cup of tea on her way.

'Not a good idea.' Lara was certain on that count. 'If I did it would only encourage him to press me to publish my story, whatever it proves to be, and I don't want that.'

She had been turning out the little spare bedroom Mrs Dunstan had used as her 'glory hole' when Michelle arrived. She had been putting off doing so because it would make her mother's death so final somehow, but once she started she had found herself smiling a lot as the contents brought back happy memories of days gone by. She had come to the bottom of the trunk where Mum had stored her sewing materials and now, sitting on the bed next to Michelle, she reached in and discovered a scrapbook.

'I bet this will be more photos of me in school plays, sports days and fancy dress!'

Mrs Dunstan had been an inveterate collector of mementoes and had a library of albums following the highs and lows of family life.

Only this one was different. For a start, Lara didn't know anyone in it.

Then there was the fact that the pictures were cut from newspapers rather than being snapshots taken with the family's trusty instant camera.

'Who's the handsome man in that

first cutting?' Michelle leaned across to get a clearer view and then, when she recognised him, exclaimed, 'Oh, it's a young Hal Lawrence, isn't it?'

Lara nodded, dumbfounded. Why would her mother collect newspaper reports on politicians?

Hal had been quite a looker, she noted, although she thought him more distinguished now that his hair was steely grey and cut in a shorter style.

Flicking over the pages she found further cuttings of Hal as a young man, and then a copy of a colour photograph from a Sunday supplement, under the headline *Rising young MP marries again*. Hal was grinning broadly, and beside him his bride, in a long golden gown and stole, smiled out — at her daughter!

Lara gasped.

She didn't realise at once, not until she read the names in the main story underneath.

Miss Chloe Peck and Mr Hal Lawrence were today married in a civil ceremony, *followed by a reception at Wyscom Old Hall.*

The article went on to mention the long association of the Lawrence family with the area, ancestors settling at the time of the Norman conquest and being lords of the manor ever since. What Mrs Dunstan's mother, who had once been in service, would have called 'minor gentry'. One newspaper, presumably one with a different political persuasion from Hal, couldn't resist some sniping comments about the groom's displaced first wife, Lady Jane Hythe, but generally the press seemed supportive of the marriage.

'That's my mother!'

Lara was shaking. She hadn't realised how much knowing who her real mother was would affect her.

'Do you think that's why Hal Lawrence sent that Dominic round?' Michelle queried. 'You said he acted as if he were his minder. Maybe he wanted to ensure your silence about an embarrassing episode in his wife's life.'

'I suppose it's possible . . . '

Dominic Leigh had been a fool, Lara thought. He should just have told her the situation and asked her to keep quiet. It was his cloak and dagger routine that had stirred her up and determined her to search for her mother.

'Do you think she'd like to hear from me?'

'Well, she might support Hal's desire to keep the past hidden. I mean, she hasn't contacted you in all this time.'

'No, but I can't really see how his wife having an illegitimate baby before they married could rebound on his career. I'd love to meet her.'

Lara felt her excitement rising as she minutely examined Chloe's face, searching for some outward sign that they were in fact related, but apart from their blonde hair, she couldn't see any likeness between them.

She turned the page and found more wedding pictures — groups this time — the magazine must have carried a complete article about the marriage. Again, she focused in on her mother, but her attention was drawn to the two bridesmaids.

'Good grief, they look just like you!' Michelle caught hold of the album and pulled it across from Lara's knee so that each of them had a page in front of them.

Even Lara could see the features she shared with them — slanting green eyes, fine bones and a well-shaped nose. She supposed Chloe's sisters had supported her on her big day and she was absurdly pleased that somewhere in the world there were people who were both related to and looked like her. It was the only thing that had bothered her about being adopted, the fact that there was no one about whom it was said, 'She looks just like Lara.' She missed that when she heard the expression used on others.

'Well, now we know why Hal doesn't want to hear from you,' Michelle said.

'I've read about his imminent appointment to some high-up post and he won't want any skeletons about his wife coming out of the cupboard at this time.'

Lara nodded. 'Approaching them both would obviously be counter-productive, so I think I'll try and find out more about my mother before doing anything. I'll look on the web after you've gone. I might be able to find a way of contacting Chloe without alerting Hal.'

★   ★   ★

However, what she found out depressed her.

Chloe and Hal Lawrence had had a child and then divorced after five years of marriage, and he had married again. After that there was plenty about Hal, but Chloe seemed to have disappeared from view, which made things difficult for Lara.

Hal clearly knew his ex-wife had had

a child outside wedlock — why else would he have sent his henchman to see her? — but for some reason, obviously felt if the fact were generally known, it could affect his campaign. Why, she couldn't imagine, but then it did seem that politicians tended to be prickly about their private lives.

Well, she was perfectly happy to promise her silence, but in exchange she wanted a contact address for her mother. She didn't want to cause any pain, but as all other avenues had drawn a blank, it became clear that approaching Hal was the only way she would be able to trace Chloe.

So, following many draft copies, she sent a short letter to her mother's ex-husband and addressed it to Wyscom Old Hall.

★　★　★

She watched the post nervously for a response and was caught completely off-guard when the doorbell rang on a

Saturday morning and she opened it to find one of the bridesmaids on her doorstep. At least, she looked like one of Chloe's attendants, but Lara realised with a shake of her head that it couldn't possibly be — not unless the girl had discovered the elixir of youth, because she hadn't aged at all.

'Good Heavens — you really are a Lawrence!'

The crystal clear vowels rang out with the easy confidence of someone who knew her place in society — and that place was the top of the pile. Red hair tumbled across her shoulders, and her casual clothes and quiet grooming could only have been achieved by someone with a great deal of money and personal style.

'I'm your sister, Henrietta Lawrence,' the girl continued.

'Half-sister,' Lara corrected as she stared in amazement at her visitor. 'I'm Chloe Lawrence's daughter, not Hal's.'

She ushered her guest into the lounge. She could see they were quite alike, and it was strange to be talking to a blood relative.

'No, no, you don't understand!' Henrietta was obviously excited. 'You — we — look like the Lawrence side of the family, not the Peck's. With your features, you have to be Hal's daughter as well as Ma's!'

Lara was stunned — she could hardly take it in. She had romanticised her birth mother as an unfortunate girl whose lover had let her down when she had presented him with a love child. To discover that in fact she had gone on to marry the man and have another child with him put a completely different complexion on the situation.

'I knew Pa was a bit of a philanderer,' Henrietta said in such a matter-of-fact way that Lara was taken aback. 'But I didn't know Ma had a past!'

'Well, she didn't really, did she?' Lara tried to keep her saintly imaginary parent from slipping away. 'There was only your father.'

'*Our* father,' corrected Henrietta, still

gazing in wonder at her sister. 'And yes, you're right, although to hear my nanny talk you'd have thought she was a scarlet woman! Nanny Blore was devoted to Pa's first wife, you see — Lady Jane, and their daughter, Hannah — but because Nanny's husband worked for Pa, she stayed in Wyscom after the divorce and looked after me when I was born.' She laughed. 'And I was never as good as Hannah, according to her!'

Lara had to know. 'What is she like?'

'Nanny Blore?'

'No, Chloe, my — *our* mother.'

Henrietta gave a quick frown and then, recognising Lara's excitement, touched her arm gently. 'Of course, you don't know, do you?' she asked softly. 'Ma died when I was four — shortly after Pa divorced her and married India.'

Lara felt as if she had been hit by a sledgehammer. Since the death of Mr and Mrs Dunstan within six months of each other, she had felt very alone, and she acknowledged that when she had discovered the identity of her birth mother she had built up an imaginary reunion where she gained a new strong and loving bond.

She felt a tear trickle down her cheek.

'Oh, don't cry!' Henrietta was horrified. Lara was to discover her sister found it hard to cope with emotions, having hers firmly under control, secure in the knowledge that her position in life made her inviolable. 'At least we've found each other. It's amazing to have an unknown sister!'

It was — and the story Henrietta told her was even more astonishing . . .

'Apparently Hal and Chloe were a real love match, whereas his marriage to Lady Jane was seen as a dynastic partnership.'

'Even in this day and age?'

'Well, not really, I suppose, but their families had been friends for years and she made a suitable politician's wife. Trouble was, Pa has always had an eye for a pretty girl, and when he met

Chloe he fell for her hook, line and sinker. If he hadn't been in politics I expect he would have kept her as his mistress and everything would have been OK, but he daren't risk it in his position — presumably especially so after you were born! So he got a divorce, married Ma, and I was born nine months later.'

'When's your birthday?'

Henrietta told her, and Lara realised she was only a year older than her sister. So by the time her adoption was finalised, Chloe must have been married to Hal, and expecting their second child.

That was when the ache began.

Until then, Lara had been happy to forgive her birth mother, to excuse their parting as a brave and noble sacrifice to ensure a better future for her daughter. Mr and Mrs Dunstan had been so wonderful to her, she had never felt she'd missed out. But to learn that it was all a lie and that, had it not been for reputation, her real parents could have kept her, made her feel worthless and unloved. And very, very angry.

Especially when her sister told her that Hal did not want to meet her.

'You must understand,' Henrietta tried to explain. 'This post he's up for is hugely important — the crowning of his entire career — and he can't risk giving his opponents any reason to question his appointment.'

Lara didn't understand. She thought it was cowardly and unkind, but she did not want to fall out with this new sister she had only just found, so she nodded her acceptance and inwardly seethed.

She wasn't asking for anything special. She merely wanted to meet the man who had given her life, to understand the little differences that had held her apart from the Dunstans, and that presumably had come from him.

Or was that really the truth? Didn't she actually want recognition — if only behind closed doors — from her father, the man who had carelessly given her

46

away and replaced her only a year later?

A little voice inside her confirmed this. Chloe was dead, which only left Hal, and whereas she once had nursed a loving feeling for a poor, abandoned unmarried mother, discovering the truth had changed her feelings for both parents. Chloe was no longer around, but Lara believed Hal owed it to her to meet her and at least try and give the reasons for what he had done.

She didn't want to shame him publicly, but she did feel she was entitled to an explanation about why he had let her go — and, what would be even more gratifying, some show of regret. She realised she was going to have to bide her time.

★　★　★

For the next six months Lara stayed on the periphery of Henrietta's life, unable to be fully included in case her real position came out. Normally she would not have accepted a situation which suggested she was something to be ashamed of, but her determination to meet Hal and hear the full story of her birth overcame her scruples, so she put up with the fleeting meetings and was pleased at the sisterly friendship that grew up between them.

'I'm so glad I misread the handwriting on the envelope as Ms H Lawrence rather than Mr, and opened your letter.' Henrietta smiled. 'Hal was away, and I was so enthralled by the idea of having a sister, I decided I had to visit you at once.'

'Even though I could've been an impostor?'

'You're forgetting how alike we are — there was no doubt when I saw the photo you sent. One look was all I needed to realise you were Chloe and Hal's love child, born while he was still married to Jane, and that you were given up for adoption.'

Lara was learning a lot from her sister.

'Pa's wonderful!' Henrietta was clearly

captivated. 'It's not his fault so many women find him irresistible. In a way, it's a shame he went into the profession he did, he'd have been much more suited to running the estate. Still, he's been very happy with India — she understands his little foibles and accepts his peccadilloes in a way that Ma never could.'

'Is that why they divorced?'

'Hmm.' Henrietta nodded. 'Of course, I can't remember any of this, but when I was older I was told Chloe wasn't prepared to play second fiddle to anyone. She couldn't take his infidelity. Hal was apparently the love of her life, and if she hadn't died in a car crash soon after they parted, her friends didn't think she would have coped with the idea of him being with India.

'India wasn't the cause of their break-up, by the way, he met her just as he divorced. He'd had a few flings while he was with Ma, but when he got divorced for the second time his political masters let it be known that if

a man in his position wanted advance-
ment he needed a suitable wife who
wouldn't go public if he was unfaithful.
India fitted the bill.'

'But if India accepts Hal's behaviour,
why doesn't he want to meet me? I
thought it was fear of exposure that was
stopping him.'

Henrietta smiled indulgently. 'The
first law of politics,' she said, 'don't get
found out! Of course, the powers that
be know about Hal playing away, but as
long as he's discreet, that's OK. And Pa
is no fool — he may admire a pretty
face, but now he only goes for women
who have their own reasons for wanting
anonymity. Chloe was the only woman
he lost his head over. His relationship
with India seems to suit them both
fine.'

She leaned over and touched Lara's
shoulder.

'It's not that he doesn't want to meet
you, it's just that there's lots of talk
today about family values, and if the
story got out that he'd abandoned you

50

as a baby, it could backfire on him. I'm sure he'll want to meet you later.'

Lara wasn't sure she would want to meet him then. He sounded so cold and calculating, and throughout all Henrietta's prattling, there had been no talk of love. She was shocked at the way in which her sister spoke about their parents and found it incomprehensible that anyone should be so accepting of infidelity and lack of commitment.

The Dunstans might not have come from so illustrious a family, but their values were sound and the greatest of these was love. Lara had felt cocooned and protected within their family, where the idea that position or self-aggrandisement should come first was totally alien.

She remembered again Malcolm's assertion that Mr Dunstan had given up a job he loved to ensure a good start for his baby. This time it filled her with loving pride. She saw her father had made the right decision, putting family before personal preferences, and knew if she ever had to make a similar choice, she would follow his lead.

Lara realised she pitied Henrietta, who had never experienced that kind of all-embracing, sacrificial love. She might have had all the material rewards that a wealthy household could give, but not the matchless gift of totally unselfish love. So when her sister became too grand, or on the occasions when she spoke carelessly about Hal and Chloe, Lara accepted it was just Henrietta's upbringing that made her that way, recognising the generous spirit that lay beneath.

She warmed to her future brother-in-law, too. Gareth was a solicitor with no pretensions of grandeur, who was resolutely unimpressed by his fiancée's forebears. He accepted Lara as soon as they met, and even said, 'Of course you must come to our wedding, they're your relatives, too!'

Henrietta Lawrence had insisted when Lara had admitted she was wary of attending, and Lara had been swept along by her sister's enthusiasm.

3

Lara knew she shouldn't have come. Attending her sister's wedding made her the problem. But she had to be here, she wanted to attend for Henrietta and to prove to her father he couldn't ride roughshod over her. But now she was here she was nervous, edgy, and she felt very alone.

The watery late September sun shone through the registry office window, falling on the burnished reds and golds of the formal flower arrangement in the corner. It was the only warmth in the room, Lara thought, eyeing the rows of utilitarian chairs around her and the plain table at the front, and she wondered again at her sister's choice of venue for such a special day in her life. Even if Henrietta hadn't wanted a church wedding, there were any number of wonderful old buildings she could have chosen instead, but she had been insistent she wanted this anonymous room on the second floor of an ugly modern council building in Middlesex.

'Nobody will be interested in anyone marrying in Cornfield, least of all the press,' she explained when Lara expressed surprise. 'I want a low-key wedding without reporters sniffing around for the latest story about Dad. It's my day, after all.'

But an odd day, Lara decided, as she looked around at her fellow guests. They all were dressed with the understated elegance that only the super-rich seemed able to achieve. Yet in spite of their finery, they didn't appear to be enjoying themselves very much. There was none of the banter and good-natured chatter she was used to at family weddings. In fact she thought the guests added to the chill of the room. She was receiving some curious glances, too, which made her feel uncomfortable and regret her decision to attend.

Sitting here among them, her courage was beginning to fail her. What had induced her to imagine this was a sensible thing to do? Why hadn't she realised how alien it would be and how different from the other guests she would feel?

But she knew the answer — she had come because she wanted to be recognised as part of the family at last, despite her father's reluctance to meet her. Typical of him, to be more concerned with his position than the bride's wishes.

Remembering her sister, she stuck her chin up defiantly. She refused to let him wind her up. After all, she had done nothing to be ashamed of. She knew people sometimes mistook her quiet demeanour to mean she was a pushover, but they soon learned their mistake. Her soft exterior hid a will of iron — as her father would find out.

She was standing at the back of the room trying to look inconspicuous, so was the first to see him enter. He was beaming with bonhomie, but when he caught sight of Lara shock registered very obviously on his face and he stopped short of the central aisle he had been heading for, whipping his head around to seek reassurance that no one had observed his reaction.

Lara faced a stranger. The familiar handsome face — blue eyes, grey hair — stared back at her, but the devastating smile had disappeared.

Her father.

'I'm so sorry.' He was more annoyed than embarrassed. 'For a moment I thought you were someone else.'

Lara didn't want to spoil her sister's day so merely smiled back and retreated to the far end of the room. Public acknowledgements had never been his style. She felt her cheeks burning, and turned to face the front again, but not before she recognised the man accompanying her father.

Even at fifty-nine Hal Lawrence's mesmerising appeal usually rendered any comparison superfluous, yet Dominic put him in the shade. His liquid eyes, with lashes that had no business being on a man, and strong, square jawline, married into a face that could certainly give Hal a run for his money. But something was missing — and that, she reluctantly allowed, was charm.

Her father had it in bucketloads, but his companion didn't flash a perfect pair of teeth at her or that most practised of all expressions — the politician's sincere smile. Rather, he raised one eyebrow quizzically and gave her such a piercing examination with those coal-black eyes that she felt he could see into her very soul.

An unwelcome frisson of excitement tingled down her spine — a mixture of anticipation and fear with an undercurrent of danger — just as it had when they first met on her doorstep, when even the fact that she was on her own home territory had not protected her from an uncomfortable awareness of this rich man's minder.

He gave her the briefest of nods and turned back to join his companion.

She was saved from further introspection by the arrival of the bride. Henrietta, like Lara, had inherited Hal's perfect bone structure, set off by translucent skin and slanting green eyes. Unlike Lara, when she smiled she also had the dazzling straight teeth that years of expensive orthodontistry had provided, and the confidence that came from being the favourite, petted child of a famous and indulgent man.

She had chosen not to wear a traditional gown.

'I'm too big to dress like a fairy,' Henrietta had said, referring to her statuesque ample curves. 'I know what I look good in, and a well designed suit will look best. And it won't attract attention when I arrive, like a wedding dress would.'

Seeing her, Lara rather doubted it. The simple straight skirt emphasised her sister's figure, and the bolero top with high collar drew attention to her swan-like neck. Her fiery red hair was piled high on her head under a striking hat, and the overall effect was both sexy and classy.

It came effortlessly to Henrietta, Lara acknowledged, years of privilege and self-esteem passing from generation to generation. Well, perhaps not passed exactly — it had missed her, after all — it was clearly more to do with nurture than with nature.

As Henrietta turned to face Gareth to exchange their vows, Lara noticed the diamond choker around her sister's throat, and a lump rose in her own. Chloe had worn the same necklace when she had married Hal — Lara had admired it in a thousand archive photographs since she had discovered her real identity.

For a moment she wondered if she would wear it when she married, and then gave herself a gentle but perceptible shake. *Don't be ridiculous!* she thought, as the registrar started the ceremony in a soft, firm voice. *Why on earth would the Lawrences lend it to you?*

She had no time for further daydreaming, because she found herself carried along on the quiet majesty of the promises Henrietta and Gareth were making to each other.

Even the sterile surroundings could not detract from the love and commitment of the main players, and Lara had to bite her tongue sharply to prevent herself from crying. She realised it would look odd for an unknown visitor to make such an exhibition of herself, so she concentrated hard on controlling her emotions and preventing the corners of her mouth from trembling.

Yet she could not deny she was deeply moved by the solemn promises and joyful expectation of the ceremony. To find the perfect partner, a soulmate who understood without being told, who loved without reservation and who you knew would never reject you — that had to be life's greatest prize.

'I want a quiet ceremony,' Henrietta had said, 'but a huge reception to make up for it!'

She had arranged for it to be held in the privacy of Hal's ancestral home in Surrey, some twenty minutes' drive from the registry office.

'I can't wait to see it,' Lara had told Michelle. 'I'm becoming very fond of Henrietta, but I was in two minds whether to accept her invitation until I heard where she was having the reception. I want to visit the place where my father grew up — where I should have done.'

'Are you sure that's wise? You've been quite shaken up by all that's happened recently. Maybe a quieter introduction would be better?'

Michelle had been the only person Lara had shared her news with, and she knew it was concern for her that made her cautious.

'Oh, Michelle — you know that since I learned about my true identity, I've been driven by this fierce need to find out why I was abandoned.'

'But Hal appears so reluctant to meet you.'

'I grant you, that makes it difficult, but I hoped that by my behaviour at the wedding, he'll see I'm not out to cause trouble, merely to find answers to my questions.' Questions that had tormented her since she'd made the shocking discovery about her parentage.

Lara had seen photographs of the small moated manor house before, of course. The garden often featured in society magazines, and was so picturesque that it had once graced a biscuit tin. But when the car she was travelling in pulled up at its destination, she still caught her breath at the scene before her.

The heavily timbered house was set with many gables and had mullioned windows that glinted as they caught the weak autumn sunshine. A wooden bridge crossed the moat, past stone walls over which tumbled late summer roses and other climbing plants.

It was almost too chocolate-boxy to be real, but on entering the house Lara saw it was not a pastiche, but a much loved and well worn home. The great hall rose from floor to roof, arching timbers echoing with the conversational buzz of the guests below. Standing at the head of the room was the bridal party.

'Lord and Lady de la Souss . . . ' The red-coated toast master intoned as the line edged forwards.

This was something Lara hadn't reckoned on, the fact that she would be introduced to and have to shake hands with her father.

Just as she was considering the point, Hal Lawrence saw her and clearly had the same thought. He turned away to confer urgently with his minder, and Lara felt herself flushing as those dark unfriendly eyes looked her up and down.

Obviously finding me wanting, she thought grimly, and then gave herself a mental shake. Just because this wasn't her usual milieu, she had no reason to feel inadequate, she reminded herself. What was it Eleanor Roosevelt had said? Something about no one being able to make you feel inferior without your consent. Well she didn't consent! As she saw Hal's henchman walking towards her, she took a deep breath and set her face in a determined expression.

★ ★ ★

Watching her, Dominic Leigh was struck by the way her cat-like green eyes narrowed and how she thrust her chin upwards at his approach, as if she was preparing to attack. He had no doubt she would do so too, if pushed. Whereas he was usually more than capable of managing the tricky situations Hal's disregard for conventional behaviour regularly caused, he suspected this one could be more difficult.

'So you came in spite of my warning, Miss Dunstan?' He extended his arm and felt her tense as they clasped hands.

'I wasn't aware I needed your permission to attend my sister's wedding when she had invited me.' She gave him a withering look.

'You don't.' He shrugged indifference. 'It would simply have been more helpful if you had kept away from the family until later in the year.'

He looked down at her, irritated by what he saw. If this had been a book, the interloper would be exposed as an impostor, and all would return to normal, but studying the girl in front of him, he knew, as he had when he'd first met her, that she was exactly who Hal had told him she was.

She shared the fine bone structure and flaring nostrils of her sister, and had the alabaster skin and almond-shaped eyes of all the Lawrence women. Her waist was neater than Henrietta's, but her hourglass figure echoed the bride's, albeit on a slighter scale. The only difference was her hair — as fair as her mother's had been

— as he could see from the fringe peeping out from under her hat.

'You'll know me again,' Lara sounded sarcastic. 'Do I pass inspection, come up to the high standards the family expects? You obviously thought I'd let them down or you wouldn't have been so opposed to my attendance.'

'I intend to get to know you better now,' he said. 'Let's give the reception line a miss.'

Without waiting for an answer he took her by the elbow and purposefully guided her through a side door, along a passageway that smelled of beeswax and lavender, past a gently ticking grandfather clock, and into a large dining room where banks of brilliant chrysanthemums set off the crisp white tablecloths.

'No one suggested you wouldn't come up to scratch.' Dominic sought to build bridges. He didn't want her angry at the reception. Angry women with a little too much champagne were likely to let rip very publicly, and he had to avoid that at all costs. 'You look — ' He paused. She looked pretty damn stunning, if the truth be told, which made his job more difficult. 'You look perfectly respectable.'

It was the wrong thing to say.

'You sound surprised. Did you assume because I hadn't been brought up as a lady that I wouldn't know how to act like one? I'm Hal's daughter after all, and what is it they say . . . breeding will out?'

'Hal's long-lost daughter . . . ' he mused.

'Not lost — I was *given away!*'

Dominic was taken aback at the intensity of her words; she fairly spat them out. He noted the firm set of her jaw and the fierce glint in those expressive sloe eyes, and he recognised trouble.

'Your parents thought they were doing the best for you — ' but again she interrupted.

'My parents didn't think of me at all! They weren't interested in giving me the best start in life. They just wanted to protect their own reputations. And judging from Hal's behaviour today, he still does!'

Dominic smiled, trying to deflect her anger. Truth to tell, he had a certain sympathy with her.

Hal might have convinced himself of the noble intent behind his actions all those years ago, but Dominic was reserving his judgement — his admiration for Hal's diplomatic skills did not blind him to what he saw as his weaknesses. The man was charismatic and wise in the ways of men and the world, but where women were concerned, he was totally self-indulgent. In his circle that was not seen as unreasonable behaviour, and Dominic knew that usually the objects of his desire understood the rules of the game and played by them, while his wife was famously 'understanding'.

But sometimes innocent people could get hurt, though he wasn't yet sure if this girl fell into that category. On the two previous occasions when they had spoken he hadn't been able to categorise her. He had wanted to believe her, but she remained an enigma.

It had not been an easy conversation when he had phoned her and tried to dissuade her from coming to the wedding.

'I don't think it's a good idea if you attend.'

'You don't think? I wasn't aware you were the spokesperson for the Lawrence family. My sister happens to think it's a very good idea.'

He had been reluctant to tell Lara the truth — that Hal didn't want to upset the bride but being unnerved at the thought of meeting his unknown daughter on such a public occasion, had pressed Dominic to try and talk her out of attending.

'Henrietta may do, but your father is not so sure. My advice — '

'I can just guess what you'll advise. Luckily, Hen doesn't kow-tow to Hal like you do!'

'Everyone will wonder who you are.'

'Hen's thought of that. She's going to put out a story about a long-lost relative.'

'Which will only serve to whet the appetites of the closer ones, who will inundate you with demands to know which branch of the family you come from.'

He shook his head. That was the last thing they needed. He'd have to get Hal to put a stop to it.

'You really have been given the job of warning me off, haven't you?' she said disparagingly.

'I'm merely suggesting you might find it rather uncomfortable. Henrietta and Gareth are the only people you'll know, and you won't be on the top table with them. How will you manage, sitting among total strangers?'

'Don't worry, guv, I was brung up proper and my table manners pass muster,' she whined in a fake Cockney accent. 'I scrub up real nice, I do.'

Facing her now, he had to agree that she did.

He gave a wry smile. Normally if he went on a charm offensive he could win over the opposite sex easily, but he had to admit that his phone call to Lara had merely made her even more determined to come to the wedding. Then she had curtly dismissed his suggestion that she might feel out of place and rung off.

However, today he had noticed in the great hall that she had been getting some pretty close stares from curious guests, most of whom knew each other and could sniff out an outsider at ten paces. He considered the woman in front of him. He still didn't know why she was here and he needed to find out.

It was important she didn't create a scene. The press might have been excluded from the wedding, but he wouldn't put it past some of the other guests to report back to political columnists if anything untoward did happen, probably accompanied by secretly snapped photos of any untoward incident. Mobile phones had a lot to answer for!

Had she come to cause trouble, he wondered, or did she want some kind of payment for her silence? He'd have to find out, but until he did, he needed to position her among people who might see the family resemblance, but who could be counted on to hold their tongues.

'Things were very different twenty years ago,' he said. 'One whiff of scandal and a politician's career would be over.'

'So I was the sacrificial lamb.'

He flicked his eyes over her.

'Isn't that a bit over the top?'

'When you've been in a similar situation, I'll consider you qualified to comment.'

Privately he acknowledged her reply was not unreasonable. It must have been a heck of a shock to find out you were the daughter of such a well known man. Hal had given him minimal details about what had transpired, but Dominic knew him well enough to recognise when something was being given the Lawrence Positive Spin.

'OK.' He propelled her across the dance floor towards the cushioned window seat that looked out over the sprawling gardens and farmland beyond. 'You sit there while I get us both a drink, and then you can tell me just what it was like.'

* * *

Lara responded to the pressure on her arm and allowed herself to be expertly eased into place. She looked down at the firm guiding hand with a mixture of surprise and annoyance.

She couldn't decide whether to be affronted or relieved by his determined intervention and wondered how the self-possessed Dominic Leigh would feel if he knew it was in no small measure down to him that she had kept her nerve and come today. No man warned her off and got away with it — especially not when using the excuse that it was for her own good.

It was true his action in the great hall had enabled her to avoid what could have proved an embarrassing situation, but the autocratic way he had led her made her hackles rise. The concept of man, the protector of fragile womanhood was alien to her, and she disliked men who automatically assumed they should take command.

Well, she did normally . . . but she had to admit there had been something oddly reassuring about his firm grip on her arm when she was feeling particularly vulnerable.

She frowned, unable to explain her jangled nerves and cursed herself for her gaucheness. Why was she behaving like a schoolgirl? And who was he to dictate what she could and couldn't do? The insolent way his piercing eyes had inspected her was disconcerting, yet she had held her shoulders back to present her best profile. What on earth was the matter with her? Why was it that ever since she'd met him she'd wanted to impress this Dominic Leigh, with his chiselled features and quizzical expression?

She stared out over the grounds. The scene before her did have a kind of timeless quality that calmed her. The garden had not yet been touched by frost, so the long borders were still a riot of bronzes and yellows and coppers and reds, the chrysanthemums and dahlias bowed but not broken by the winds autumn had thrown at them. Beyond the formal garden, sculptural branches in the shrubbery were laden with berries, their feet clothed with swathes of autumn crocus. A little to the left was a distant view of ploughed brown earth. The ancient window did not fit the oak frame as snugly as it might, so she could hear the cawing of the circling rooks in the fiery beech trees that edged the fields, and there was the smell of wood smoke in the air.

So unlike her small city house, and

yet somehow familiar. Was this collective memory, a shared family history imprinted on her brain even before birth? She had been so young when she had left Wyscom, yet she felt as if she was returning home.

But home was in North London . . .

Staring out over the autumn landscape, Lara remembered being both nervous and excited by the invitation, determined she would blend into the surroundings so no one would make the connection. She wouldn't embarrass Hal. But she'd hoped he would approach her.

That was what made Dominic's guard dog stance so galling. Did he really imagine she would do anything to spoil her sister's big day? To discover a long lost sister had been such a joy, she would never jeopardise their relationship — not even to talk to Hal.

4

Dominic handed her a crystal flute before sitting down at the far end of the window seat. 'Penny for them?'

'I was thinking about how Hen and I first met.'

'I was surprised when I learned how she came down to sound you out.'

He remembered how furious Hal had been when he'd found out. The man might be unconventional, but normally he was too much the politician to involve his family in any situations that could rebound on his career. It had been far more his style to get Dominic to find out what his correspondent wanted.

'She was intrigued,' Lara said.

He raised his eyebrows. He liked Henrietta, but was aware she had developed the same acute antennae as her father as far as potentially damaging stories in the press were concerned. Like many families in the public eye, self-preservation was the name of the game, and it was not very politically astute to have gone running off to visit a stranger who claimed to be her sister without doing any checking first.

Lara seemed to read his thoughts — that he didn't trust her and was surprised Henrietta had done so.

'I'd sent a photograph of myself, and she recognised the likeness,' she said simply, 'although I had thought it was through Chloe, so it was a shock to find out I actually look like the Lawrences.'

She did, too, he thought, and they were all remarkably good-looking women, although he had never been physically attracted to one before.

Dominic was acutely aware of her closeness next to him on the seat, her pale skin and perfect features proclaiming a cool aristocrat, yet her plain speaking approach to life suggesting someone far earthier.

He looked down at her, and was both

surprised and amused by the stirrings the view roused in him. It had been many years since he'd felt like this — not since he was an inexperienced young man not yet master of his own emotions, though that had come with time.

That, he knew, was how he differed from Hal. Whereas he was always in control in any relationship, the politician was a victim of his own passions. In Dominic's opinion it was often others, like this girl, who suffered most as a result of Hal's behaviour, so perhaps they were the real victims.

He nodded his understanding.

'But you seem to have hit it off?'

'We have. Henrietta had always wanted a sister her own age. She had Hannah, of course, but they weren't very close. Five years is a big age gap when you are children and they were brought up in different families.'

'As were you and Hen.'

'Yes, but we didn't know about each other, so there was no jealousy. We just enjoyed getting to know one another. We're very alike in many ways, as I'm sure you and a number of others will have noticed today.'

So that was her game. Up until that moment, Dominic had felt a certain sympathy for the lovely girl beside him, the love child of Hal and Chloe. In the great hall she had looked out of her depth and lonely without her sister at her side, but he was too old a hand not to recognise her veiled threat. She knew her face was all the proof she needed as to her real identity, and there were plenty of magazines that would jump at the chance to publish her story.

She couldn't have chosen a worse time to turn up, either, with Hal about to be confirmed as lead negotiator around some very contentious issues in Europe.

Dominic frowned. Whatever the failings of his private life, Hal was a skilled diplomat, and the general consensus was that he was one of the few people who could carry off the role and really make a difference. But there were factions who wanted him to fail, and who were determined to use all means available to them to sabotage the delicate balance of power.

Some of the countries involved were more rigid in their approach to the behaviour they expected of those in public life — what better weapon for them than the disclosure of an abandoned child on the eve of Hal's appointment?

* * *

Lara sensed his anger simmering just below the surface, and realised he did not welcome her friendship with Henrietta. Not surprising, really, if as a result he was going to be expected to keep her away from Hal — she'd recognised when he ushered her from the receiving line that he was acting on her father's orders.

It looked as if Dominic would be dogging her footsteps to ensure their paths didn't cross.

For a moment she indulged herself with the image of him shadowing her, just in reach but never quite touching, and was startled by the pang of regret she felt when she pulled herself back to reality and the knowledge that it wasn't going to happen.

She was sure the man beside her, who exuded such a sense of raw power, could find a much more efficient method of control if he so chose. He seemed to fill the whole expanse of the window seat, invading her space and making her very aware of his presence.

People began to file into the dining room to find their places on the seating plan. Her companion gave her an enquiring look, and then approached the major domo orchestrating the tables.

'Miss Dunstan and I will sit together, Reader,' he said pre-emptively. 'Over there, I think.'

'Very good, Mr Leigh,' the man nodded, and escorted them to where

Dominic had indicated, some distance from the top table.

Lara glared at him. 'Are you trying to hide me, Mr Leigh?'

She felt her hackles rising. He was exhibiting all the overbearing attributes that Malcolm had displayed, although she had to admit, his air of quiet authority was quite different from her cousin's approach.

And there was something more. In spite of his relaxed stance, she was sure that underneath there was a core of steel only just held at bay which he would not hesitate to use if she protested too loudly.

'I'm sure that's not something you're used to,' he drawled, 'men making you hide yourself.'

Lara bristled, sure he meant it as an insult.

It was totally untrue — she didn't dress to attract attention. In fact she loathed men who seemed only able to address her chest and had a collection of acid put-downs to force their eyes elsewhere. Yet, in spite of Dominic's penetrating gaze, she didn't use one now — and she couldn't have said why not.

* * *

Dominic dismissed his sudden sense of disappointment as the normal reaction of any red-blooded male. It was not in his nature to ogle women, however gorgeous. Indeed, sometimes he had been on the receiving end of such visual messages himself. There had been plenty of women whose sultry stares had made it plain they'd be only too happy to get to know him better.

He didn't take the offers up. If they made it to him they could do so to others, and he knew only too well the absolutes he demanded of any relationship — fidelity and, above all, trust.

He pulled out a chair for Lara, and expertly helped her to take her seat, before placing himself firmly beside her. She was too dangerous to leave to her own devices, and not simply because of her hidden past. If her physical attributes had drawn him to her — and he admitted they had in spite of both his experience and the cynicism that mixing with the rich and powerful had given him — how much more potent could they be with the susceptible? He would have to stay close to her to keep inquisitive others at bay, and he had to confess his responses were telling him that it might not be such an onerous assignment.

★ ★ ★

They were joined on their table by a number of elderly family retainers, and Lara realised that Dominic's seemingly quick reorganisation of the seating plan had not simply been a matter of getting her as far away from Hal as possible. By ensuring she only chatted with faithful pensioners there was less chance her presence would be detected and cause embarrassment.

Yet she was enjoying herself, and realised that by his meddling, Dominic had actually made the situation easier for her. Neither she nor Henrietta had thought things through when agreeing Lara's attendance at the wedding breakfast, but now she acknowledged that being placed among her sister's friends might have proved tricky. She imagined the stilted conversation that could have arisen with people she didn't know and wondered how on earth she would have answered if asked what her connection was to the bride or groom.

At least her present companions did not require her to say anything about herself, their respectful conversation echoing a lifetime in service where discretion was their watchword.

For all but Nanny Blore, that was.

'Isn't a patch on Hannah's wedding,' she sniffed. 'But then, her mother was a Lady, and you can't fake that sort of class.'

The rest of the party looked scandalised, and Lara found it hard not to giggle. That anyone should still think in those archaic terms was crazy to her, but the shocked expressions on the faces around her showed these people still stuck to the rigid definitions of class. She admired Nanny's forthrightness, though she suspected it had more to do with approaching dementia than rebellion.

'Miss Henrietta looks lovely.' Mrs Greene, who had introduced herself to Lara as a former housekeeper, valiantly tried to change the subject. Lara was sure the woman's sharp eyes had made the connection between her and Hal, but the housekeeper was too steeped in deferential obsequiousness to her former employer to comment on it. 'Just like her dear mother.'

So Mrs Greene had known Chloe! Lara leaned forward hoping to learn more.

'Handsome is as handsome does.' Nanny was not to be deflected. 'Breaking up a happy family — well, you reap what you sow in this life.'

There was an embarrassed silence, broken by the toastmaster announcing the speeches. Lara wanted to listen but found instead she was thinking of Henrietta's mother — her mother. The woman against whom Nanny Blore seemed to harbour such a deep resentment. The woman she had once believed had paid heavily for a single mistake — having to give up her love child before she had met and married Hal — until Henrietta had disabused her of that fairytale.

How could they have discarded her in that way, without a thought? No matter how hard she tried to consider the story rationally, Lara could not get away from the fact that both her parents had thought her expendable.

Even today Hal avoided her like the plague. Well, she would make him acknowledge her existence, even if she couldn't make him admit regret. She had no thought about 'paying him back' so she would ensure there was no publicity about their relationship, but she *did* want his recognition.

If that put her on a collision course with his minder, so be it! She would enjoy putting the arrogant Mr Leigh in his place.

To be fair, he'd had his uses today. She might have been looking forward to the wedding, but now she was here she wasn't so sure it had been a good idea. In spite of her determination to blend into the surroundings so no one would make the connection, things might have got out of hand without Dominic hiding in this corner where her likeness to the Lawrences would not be commented upon. Although she was annoyed by the knowing way he had stage-managed her, she had noticed the questioning looks some of the guests nearer the high table had given her, and accepted that keeping her out of sight was probably a sensible precaution.

She didn't intend to tell him so, though. She turned and gave him a cold stare, and was disconcerted when he returned an infuriating grin.

The speeches were over, and although Hal had spoken at length, Lara was unable to recollect one thing he had said. All the time the thought raced around her head — *he's my father!* In spite of her good intentions, she was crestfallen that he had not even wanted to shake her hand, and her disappointment showed on her face.

Dominic was watching her closely, as if determined to leap at the first sign of gossip, though she couldn't understand why he appeared so tense and buttoned up. Although Mrs Greene was watching her too, the rest of the pensioners did not appear to have made the connection.

'Dance?'

It might have been couched as a question, but it brooked no chance of refusal, and Lara realised he felt it best to get her away from the table where she could be scrutinised, and onto the dance floor where the lights were dimmed.

She liked dancing, and knew she moved well. She turned to face her partner, and gyrated and swayed in time with the music. *Bother Hal Lawrence and bother his minion!* she thought. She wasn't going to let them see how much she had hoped for her father's acceptance today.

Her hips swayed rhythmically, and she shook her shoulders as the beat increased. Dominic looked furious. She obviously was drawing too much attention to herself for his liking, in spite of his guiding her towards the shadows of the crowded dance floor. His face was thunderous, and a pulse on the line of his neck beat ominously. His eyes were hooded and dangerous, and disdainfully followed the gleams of perspiration that she could feel trickling down her neck.

Lara noted his discomfort with satisfaction. *Put that in your pipe and smoke it!* she thought childishly. *People are noticing me because of my dancing, not because of who I might be!*

The number ended, and the band moved smoothly into a slow ballad. She turned to return to her seat, sure he would not want to spend another minute with her, but her wrist was caught in a vice-like grip.

He murmured in her ear, 'This is one of my favourites. Now we'll dance *my* way.'

Powerful arms pulled her body close to his, and she gasped as she felt his lean and muscular form mould to the fullness of her figure. She was astonished by the contraction of her stomach that this sudden physical contact caused — after all she was a regular dancer, but never before had she experienced such a sensation. He guided her around the dance floor, his long, immaculately trousered legs forcing hers to follow where he led.

* * *

She smelled of jasmine and joie de vivre, and at that moment he could happily have eaten her! He'd been annoyed when she'd drawn attention to herself with her dancing, and then annoyed with himself because he was honest enough to accept his anger had been about more than Lara undermining Hal's position. That was why he had pulled her close to him in an act of ownership that kept inquisitive eyes at bay. He gazed down at her and again he felt that disquieting but enjoyable stirring. He needed to get a grip on himself!

It was all an act, of course. Lara wanted to win him over, he was sure of that, and thought that by getting him on her side she would have a way in to Hal. He ought to disabuse her of that belief right now, but he doubted she'd listen. In which case, he would have to hold back. He didn't want the situation to get more complicated than it already was and, however attractive she was, he needed to distance himself.

He was surprised at how depressing he found his decision. Heaven knew he was used to predatory women and had learned the hard way how necessary it was to avoid their wiles. Why should Lara be any different?

Perhaps because initially he had felt sorry for her — had imagined she was upset by what she saw as the desertion of her original family — but her behaviour now proved Hal had seen things more clearly. She was an exhibitionist, and as such, likely to want to see herself gracing the news. He would have to keep a tight rein on her, at least until Hal was confirmed in post. After that, she could tell who she jolly well pleased!

★　★　★

The music faded, and he dropped his arms and let her go as if she were something rather nasty that the cat had brought in, Lara thought.

On one level, it was a relief, but on another, she had to admit she had enjoyed herself. It was so unsettling

— why had she not felt like this when she had danced with other men before?

She remembered the boyfriends who had held her tightly and kissed her, and from whom she had quickly withdrawn when it looked as if they might want more. Then, it had never been a hardship — but today . . .

Was this what Chloe had experienced — an attraction that had made her Hal's plaything? She felt mildly ashamed at her inability to manage her own feelings, but at least she had an explanation for her uncharacteristic behaviour — heredity!

And now she knew how dangerous Dominic Leigh was to her equilibrium, she would try to give him a wide berth in future — especially when carrying out her plan to challenge Hal.

Having inadvertently drawn attention to herself with her exuberant dancing, Lara wasn't surprised when Dominic didn't take her onto the floor again and was amused by the possessiveness he displayed to keep prospective dance partners at bay. The trouble was, his very monopolisation was drawing attention.

She wondered what stories people were imagining about the handsome minder and the outsider who looked so much like the Lawrences. Assuming she was the result of a romp on the wrong side of the blankets by a Lawrence man with a female member of staff, no doubt, thinking how sweet it was that she had attracted the attention of someone so suited to her station in life — Hal's right-hand man, but a servant nevertheless.

She didn't care, and in the absence of any further conversation from her table companions, she made do with surreptitiously watching her father across the room.

Hal was in his element, in his own home, surrounded by friends, good food and beautiful women. His wife, India, the woman whom Henrietta had told her was able to turn a blind eye to her husband's roving one, sat beside him. She was about twenty years younger than he, and they'd had no children, although according to Henrietta, she had been a kind stepmother. She smiled indulgently as her husband took centre stage, and Lara watched, fascinated by this unknown parent who lived a life so alien to the faithful, suburban one she had known.

'I'll drive you home,' Dominic abruptly interrupted her thoughts.

'I'll get a taxi, thank you.' The last thing she wanted was to be alone with him.

'No you won't.' He dismissed her reply. 'I'll get the car brought round and then fetch you.'

'Impossible man!' Lara glared after his departing figure.

'Yes, he is, isn't he?'

She hadn't realised she had said it aloud and turned to find India Lawrence had taken his seat beside her.

'I'm India Lawrence,' she said unnecessarily, 'and you're Lara.'

Momentarily Lara was surprised her

identity was known, but quickly realised that of course, within the privacy of the family, she would have been talked about.

'Dominic can be quite impossible, but he's nice all the same.' India smiled.

'To your family, maybe — and useful as well, I suppose.'

Lara was so sure Dominic had been sent to 'manage' her, she threw caution to the wind. Who were these people to try and run her life? They hadn't been interested when she was baby, after all.

'To everyone, I find. Oh, he doesn't suffer fools gladly, but that can be a blessing when you're in a position of authority and are surrounded by yes men. He's very good for Hal.'

'I'm sure he is.' Lara dripped sarcasm. After all, most servants were good for their employers; that was why they were employed. 'He makes an excellent minder — keeping me at bay.'

India Lawrence had a friendly face, and she flashed Lara an amused smile. 'Is that how it feels? Oh, dear.'

She turned away from the table so Lara could hear her, but her table companions could not.

'Dominic supports Hal's belief that the only way we'll overcome the problems that lie ahead is by negotiation, and he thinks the best man for the job is Hal.' She saw Lara's sceptical look and smiled. 'Yes, you're right,' she said as if Lara had spoken. 'Hal's something of a lady's man and doesn't always behave as he should, but in all the years we've been married, he has always come home to me.'

Her grey eyes looked triumphant as she made this last comment, and at once Lara understood how much it had cost Hal's wife to overlook his wanderings.

'And ability as a diplomat is not predicated on perfect domestic arrangements.'

'In which case, I can't understand why he won't meet me.'

'He will, once he's in post,' India assured her just as Henrietta had done.

'At the moment he doesn't want anything to rock the boat, that's all. And he's not just thinking of himself — he really does believe in what he is doing, and if he loses out, he will be letting down a lot of people who are relying on him. That's why I'm asking you to be a bit circumspect, just for another month, until everything is settled. Will you?'

Would she? Well, of course she would. It had never been her intention to make a fuss, anyway. Initially all she had wanted was to trace her mother. It was only when she discovered who her father was and how he had behaved that she had decided she would make him appreciate exactly what he had done — make him concede it was wrong, even if only to her.

She deserved more than being banished to a back table at a family wedding, but truth to tell, the more she heard about him, the less sure she became that she wanted anything to do with him.

Again, India seemed to understand.

'It takes a very strong man to risk everything for his child,' she said gently. 'Hal is a skilled politician, a good man in many ways, but not a great man, because he counts the cost. And yes, he's ashamed of what he and Chloe did all those years ago, simply to protect themselves, but not so ashamed that he will put everything on the line for you now. Even today it is all too easy for a man to walk away from his offspring.'

She rose as Dominic approached.

'I look forward to seeing you again,' she said, and was gone.

5

Dominic led her to where his car was waiting. It was an expensive sporty number, and he seemed to enjoy her discomfort as she struggled gamely to enter discreetly, towering over her as she slid her long legs round to the front, and smiling as she doubled forward. He shut the door and climbed easily into the driver's seat, before roaring off down the drive.

'So, did you enjoy the wedding?' he asked as they turned onto the motorway for London.

'It was . . . interesting,' Lara decided. 'A bit too grand and unfriendly for me.'

'I thought you were very friendly when you were dancing.' He gave her a lingering glance before turning his attention back to the road. 'There were any number of men who appreciated your lack of inhibition.'

Stung; she retorted without thinking, 'I didn't notice you turning your back!'

'No, but then, I wasn't meant to, was I? The whole routine was meant for me.'

Lara was sure her mouth must have dropped open. How conceited could a man be? And what kind of girl did he think she was? She had danced because she loved to, and it certainly hadn't been for his benefit!

Or had it? She had to admit that once the slow number had started and he took her in his arms she had entered a different world, and perhaps her movements thereafter had been geared towards pleasing him. Or was it pleasing herself? And what did that make her?

She blushed and said nothing.

He gave a supercilious smile and turned the radio on low. Lara decided that discretion was the better part of valour, so she gave him her address and then closed her eyes, feigning sleep. At least that way she wouldn't have to talk to him. In fact her eyes did feel heavy, and the unfamiliar champagne had gone to her head. She snuggled deeper into the bucket seat and luxuriated as the powerful machine ate up the miles in the dark of the night.

★   ★   ★

Glancing down at her, Dominic thought how in sleep she presented as a different woman from the uptight one he had met at the wedding. Her body was completely relaxed and open; in her slumbering state she had lost the protective barriers she had put up. She looked softer now, and he found himself judging her less harshly than he had. It must have been a shock to find out she was a Lawrence, and Hal's behaviour today had hardly been fatherly.

Perhaps a scandal could be avoided. He hoped so. Lara hadn't been treated well and he empathised with her; told

105

himself that was why he'd felt drawn to her. But he had to be careful — it could all be an act. He prided himself that he did not repeat mistakes. Only once had he allowed himself to be used by a woman, and that had been years ago. He had learned his lesson well and didn't intend to go down that path again.

* * *

Lara awoke as the car finally pulled up outside her house. She struggled to get out of the deep bucket seat, and felt his hand under her elbow as he stood by the passenger door, assisting her to her feet. Again, that same fizz of excitement she had experienced at the wedding. She felt somewhat embarrassed by her reaction, but also curious. She was beginning to understand what it was Mrs Dunstan had warned her against and why — the strength of her emotions had caught her by surprise.

'I hope you will keep a low profile until after Hal has been installed in his new post?'

It was pleasantly said, but Lara heard the underlying warning in his tone and it made her angry. She had already recognised he was a man with a steel centre when crossed — hard and cold — who was used to getting what he wanted.

'I'll talk to whomever I want, about whatever I want, and whenever I want. Thank you for the lift.'

She turned and walked towards her front door.

★ ★ ★

Dominic stood still for a few moments, planning his next move. He prided himself on his clear analytical brain, so was dismayed to find that even while he was trying to decide on the best course of action, he kept seeing Lara's tantalisingly inviting slumbering form in his front seat. He knitted his brows together, recognising the danger in thinking he could play a woman like Lara along.

He'd known a number of what he called good-time girls, women who were prepared to offer themselves for what they perceived as a good return, but he had only been caught once. Now he made sure he was always the winner because he was always in control — he could take it or leave it.

Whereas with Lara, he knew it would be different. In spite of being only too aware of what she was really after, he could see she could become as addictive as a drug, something he would need regularly in larger and larger doses to satiate his desire to get to know her better.

He took a deep breath.

He intended to manage her for the next four weeks, just to ensure Hal got his chance — but he'd have to be careful. Very careful indeed.

★　★　★

Lara found it hard to sleep that night. Partly because of the champagne — having sent her to sleep in the car, she was then wide awake until the early hours of the morning. But mostly it was due to her constantly reliving her exchanges with Dominic. She tried to push them out of her mind, but they would rise without warning, nudging her to remember not only the words that were used but also the emotions she had experienced.

And that was her downfall. For no matter how much she chided herself as a fool and told herself it was simply hormones, she remained curiously fascinated by him. She wished she could wipe her memory clean, but then questioned if she would do so even if she had the ability. Did she want to lose the memory of those emotions, or was it merely her reaction to it she wished to forget?

She was glad she didn't have to work the next day. She had taken leave when she had been told the wedding date, secure in the knowledge that her partner, Madge Holt, could hold the fort, and she still had a few days to go before she was due to start a new contract with a firm of stockbrokers in the City of London.

She had been flattered when Madge had asked her if she'd like to go into partnership in setting up the agency three months ago — the older woman had years of experience and would only have chosen someone she really trusted. But it was still a bit scary. She had raised a large mortgage on the house to put in her share of the money, and wondered how her cautious parents would have reacted had they known.

Things were going well so far, with a number of excellent temps choosing to work for them, although Lara still needed to undertake some of the jobs herself while Madge ran the agency. She didn't mind, she liked temping; the variety suited her, and as one of the top personal assistants on the agency's books, she got interesting jobs.

One day, when the agency was more secure, she'd give it up and join Madge in the office full time, but for now she was happy to do what was necessary to make the venture a success.

She planned to pamper herself prior to her new job, and the day before she was due to start, booked a day at a health club, where she was scrubbed and pummelled and stroked with oils and perfumes, before returning home with her body feeling reborn, but her mind still as confused as ever.

There was a message on her answerphone from Madge, asking her to ring back.

'Lara, oh, thank goodness!' Madge sounded relieved. 'Change of plan, dear. We've just been offered a really lucrative contract with Allied Markets — you know, the huge distribution company — and we've no one available. It has to be someone we trust absolutely — first impressions count for so much, and as a new client, we need to impress them. So I thought of you.'

'Oh? But I'm booked to go to Mallard's.'

'Were booked, dear. I've spoken to their office manager, and they were quite happy to take Lucy Dean — remember her, the girl who has to support her ailing mum?'

How could I forget? thought Lara wryly. *You wheel her out as the excuse whenever you want to change my schedules.*

But all she said was a non-committal, 'I see.'

She wasn't desperate to go to Mallards, and she knew Madge was the senior partner, but she did like to have some say over what she did.

Madge seemed to sense the guarded response.

'I understand Allied are a wonderful firm to work for,' she rushed on, 'and of course, it's a great feather in our cap getting them, as they usually prefer to employ permanent staff or use their own bank of people. Getting them on board will help secure our future, so

112

long as we can send them the right person, of course.'

'Emotional blackmail.'

'What?'

'You heard.' Lara was exasperated but not cross. She knew Madge had a sixth sense about which secretary would fit best where, but she didn't usually change things at this late date. Still, if it was best for the company, she wasn't going to argue. Allied Markets were pretty big business, and according to the financial press their European branches were doing very well.

'OK,' she said, grabbing a pencil and pad. 'Give me the gory details.'

★   ★   ★

She dressed carefully on Wednesday. She knew some people thought a personal assistant was the lowest form of life, one step up from the office junior, but that didn't bother her. She might have started with good word processing ability alone, but over the years had developed her talents, and now had an impressive array of computer skills, as well as what Madge liked to describe as emotional intelligence.

Put simply, Lara liked people, and wanted to help them, and as she had matured, she had learned what motivated people at work and what made them dig their heels in, and used this to good advantage when managing the offices of busy organisations.

She was also aware that people tended to make snap assessments of new staff — within forty-five seconds of meeting them one trainer had told her — so she ensured her appearance was smart, efficient and non-threatening.

For her first day at Allied Markets she chose a plain green suit which accentuated her eyes, and applied just enough make-up to show she had made an effort without looking as if it would be a terrible shock for everyone if she took it off.

She travelled by bus rather than the

Tube, even though this meant making two changes. She enjoyed riding on the top deck and admiring views usually hidden at pavement level. With a sudden flash of self-awareness, she realised she didn't like things to be obscured, which could be why she was finding her position with the Lawrences so difficult. The Dunstans had been so transparent in all their dealings that she was uncomfortable with the subterfuge forced upon her, and disliked the idea that she was something to be ashamed of and hidden away.

Allied Markets was housed in a modern block close to the Thames, and although it was still called Markets House, Lara learned that because of out-sourcing, most of the floors of the tall building were now let out to other businesses, although the company retained use of the ground floor and also the penthouse suite.

'Hi, I'm Helen Purvis,' the head of personnel told her when she arrived. 'You'll be on the top floor where our chief executive officer has his offices.' She eyed Lara curiously. 'It was he who insisted we go to Holt's for his temporary PA. His own is on maternity leave, but we've been managing perfectly well using different girls from our own pool of temporary staff. We've never used an agency before.'

Lara smiled and nodded her head. She knew better than to be drawn into office politics, especially on her first day. She was a professional, her qualifications were good, and she wasn't a gossip. Anyway, Madge had given her no idea why their agency had been chosen.

'I'll take you up to your office,' Helen said, and led the way to the private lift that raced without stopping to the top floor. 'Now that we only have the two floors in our use, it's quicker to have an express lift.' She ushered Lara into a spacious office with ergometric furniture, state of the art equipment, and a panoramic view of London.

'It's beautiful!' Lara had worked in

some pretty swish offices in her time, but the view of the capital from this one set it apart.

'Yes,' agreed her companion, 'but I must warn you, you won't have time to admire it. The boss is a hard taskmaster, and it's pretty much nose to the grindstone for everyone in the company, though you will have an assistant. Her name is Jane Power, and she's good as long as you spell out exactly what you want her to do. You may have to go on business trips, so it's important you leave things so Jane is able to hold the fort for a few days.'

'I'm not afraid of work.' Lara inclined her head with a smile. 'When do I get to meet Jane and the boss?'

'I'll send Jane up — her office is on the ground floor, which is a bit of a bind for her but no real problem. The CEO will be in later today, but he's left you some dictation on the audio tape to be getting on with. Good luck!' And she was gone.

Lara walked around the office,

getting a feel for where everything was and marking her territory so she could just slide into her usual, efficient routine each morning.

She had no time for hot-desking, having seen how long it took staff to make the area 'theirs' whenever they sat in a new position, and was aware she needed to feel at home in her space before she could settle down.

She met Jane at ten o'clock, and was pleased to find she liked her assistant, although she could see what Helen Purvis had meant; the girl was keen but would need careful instruction. She set her some work to do and then settled down to deal with what the CEO had left for her.

At eleven o'clock she went to get a coffee from the machine on the ground floor. Half an hour later she had returned to her desk and was typing away furiously when a voice crackled over the intercom and made her jump:

'Come in, please, Miss Dunstan.'

Her new boss must have come into

the office when she had taken her break. She picked up a pad and pencil and knocked on the walnut door that separated her office from his.

'Enter!'

She turned the handle and walked in.

The room was larger than hers, with a giant desk overlooking the Thames, walls lined with books and files. In one corner was a comfortable seating area with two couches and a glass-topped coffee table.

The boss was standing with his back towards her, studying the view. The bright and unseasonable October sunshine threw him into shadow, and she shaded her eyes to see more clearly.

'Sit down,' he said, waving his hand towards the sofas, and although she made towards them, she frowned, as something nagged at her as being not quite right. She went to the far sofa and turned to sit down at exactly the same time as her new boss turned from the window to face her.

The shock was so great that her

knees buckled under her and she practically fell into the soft leather cushions.

'You!' was all she could utter.

The amused face of Dominic Leigh smiled at her sardonically.

'As you so eloquently put it,' he said mockingly, 'Me!'

6

Dominic Leigh walked towards her, his broad shoulders and well-toned body carelessly elegant in a grey pinstriped suit that fairly shrieked money. His eyes were as dark and as hard as rain-soaked slate, and she felt her mouth go dry as he flashed her a look of utter disapproval.

'Why are you here?' she demanded, feeling at a distinct disadvantage.

'It's my office.' He was amused by her confusion.

'No, it isn't — it's the CEO's!' But already she was beginning to fear a plot.

'Yes,' he smiled, 'and I'm the CEO.'

'No you're not! You work for Hal.' She glowered at him as he sat opposite her, his long torso dwarfing her even in the seated position.

'Whatever made you think that?' he quizzed her, an infuriating half smile hovering on his lips.

'You told me — '

'I think you'll find you were the one who said I worked for Hal, not me. I merely refrained from correcting you. As a businessman, I know how important it is that we retain close ties with our European colleagues as we move forward, so I support Hal in his endeavours. But I work for myself, not as Hal's employee.'

His amused tones made Lara flush as she remembered how she had assumed his position on the servants' table at the wedding had been earned by his employment.

If only she had researched the company more closely before she had come! Normally she found out as much as she could about any prospective employers, going online to read annual reports and financial accounts so she could hit the ground running on her first day. If she had done so with Allied Markets, she would have realised who ran the company and could have declined the assignment.

However, just as quickly as she thought this, she realised Dominic had had it all arranged. It hadn't been by chance that Madge had only phoned her up at the last minute, he must have planned to make sure everything was done in such a rush that she wouldn't have time to make the usual enquiries. She wondered what yarn he had spun Madge to ensure he got her.

'So why am I here?' she demanded.

'I should have thought that was obvious.' He feigned surprise. 'I need a good PA, your company provides good PAs, ergo, here you are.'

'You know what I mean!'

Her surprise was giving way to annoyance. Not another man who wanted to run her life! First Malcolm and now Dominic — and neither of them really wanted her, it was what she was worth to them that mattered. To Malcolm she was the chance of a major scoop in the national papers, and to Dominic . . . well actually, she realised, she didn't really know what he wanted. Except that it certainly wasn't her, for herself.

What was his angle and why was she here? She had no doubt this was a put-up job, but for the life of her she couldn't see why.

He explained, 'I don't intend to let you ruin the one chance we have of settling the European problem simply because you feel life has treated you unfairly.'

So Hal was behind it all, which showed that even if Dominic didn't work for her father, he was nevertheless very closely involved with his political life. Why else would a successful businessman go out of his way to employ someone he had only too clearly demonstrated he didn't trust?

'Hal may not have been the best parent a girl could've wished for,' Dominic continued, 'but he wasn't the worst, either, and there's no doubt it could be damaging to him if it got out. Not because what he did was so heinous — lots of babies were given up for adoption when you were born — but because unscrupulous people can, by hint and innuendo, distort the truth and make it sound a thousand times worse than reality.'

'What has that got to do with me?'

'You're a loose cannon.' His eyes were mistrustful. 'I don't know what you might do. By having you with me as my PA for the next few weeks, I can protect Hal and the important work he is going to do.'

Now she was really angry!

'Well, I've got news for you — I'm not going to play your game! How dare you try and control me! You know nothing about me, so let me tell you, there isn't enough money in the world to induce me to work for a big bully like you!'

She rose shakily to her feet, cheeks aflame, green eyes wide with fury. She made to stride to the door, but Dominic swiftly blocked her way, caught her wrists and held them tightly. She struggled against him, her mouth set hard over clenched teeth, and he knew he had to make her obey his commands.

As he grabbed her, Lara cursed under her breath, fighting to prevent him pinning her arms to her sides.

'I'm really rather enjoying your struggling.' Dominic was sure if he told her to stop she would fight all the more, so he used the one weapon that would get through to her. She stopped at once, and reluctantly he set her free. She made towards the door.

'Before you go, hear me out,' he said quickly. 'Your agency already has a good reputation, but it's a very new company, and if it ever lost credibility, that would be the end of it.'

She stopped in her tracks and turned back.

He sauntered towards her.

'If a company like Allied Markets spread the word that they had been let down at the last minute, it would be very bad for the agency. Other companies would question whether it was advisable to do business with you, and rival agencies would line up to poach your staff.' He gave her an insufferably superior smile. 'But if you stay, I'll make sure all our business goes your way in the future and that you personally get the reference of your career.'

Lara could barely speak she was so livid.

'That's blackmail!' she spat out. 'And I don't need your reference. If you are prepared to give me one without even knowing what my work is like, I'm surprised you haven't bankrupted the company and been sacked!'

'It's hard to sack the owner,' he said glibly. 'And actually I do know.' His eyes gleamed as if amused by her discomfort. 'I may be fond of Hal, but I'm not a fool. I researched you very carefully before approaching your part- ner — and no, she wasn't in on it — just put her agreeing to move you around down to my undoubted charm! I'm sure you'll do me admirably. We both know that you're too proud to do a less than perfect job, don't we? Now . . . are you staying?'

Her mind was in a whirl. The owner — of all this? She gave a shake of her head as if to clear it.

Still, why should she be surprised that someone who moved in the same circles as Hal also had the same advantages of privilege and inherited wealth? Or that his values were so very like her father's, as shown by his arrogant assumption that he had the right to dictate to her what she would do. Inwardly she seethed at the power that money gave him, because she knew when she was beaten. She might loathe the man and all he stood for, but she couldn't risk damaging the agency.

'All right,' she said, 'but I don't want to spend one minute longer with you than I have to!'

'Beautifully put.' He gave her the ghost of a smile. 'Now let's get on, shall we?'

She glared at him, knowing she had no choice.

Even as she agreed to his terms, she was identifying a way to make the situation work for her. More than anything she wanted Hal's acknowledgement of her as his daughter — she accepted that now. True, when she was first searching for her origins she would have been happy simply to meet her birth parents, but her father's behaviour had changed all that. Why should he get away with treating women as a changeable commodity, and children as disposable assets?

She didn't want revenge exactly, but she had a strong sense of what was right and wrong, and she felt he ought to be ashamed and feel some remorse for his previous actions. India had said he did. Well, she wanted him to look her straight in the eye while he said the words to her himself and asked for her forgiveness. Not publicly — that would be asking too much — but privately, to her.

That he didn't want any such occasion to arise was evident from his persuading Dominic to employ her and keep her away from him. Well, two could play that game. However much she disliked the arrogant businessman in front of her, she had been given the perfect opportunity to prove to him that she was no money-seeking chancer, but a respectable and principled woman.

* * *

In spite of her fine plans, she did not at first find it easy working for Dominic Leigh, her hackles rising every time he told her what to do. But soon her innate professionalism took over, and she began to enjoy her work.

Against her better judgment, she was impressed with the way Dominic worked. She discovered that he was, as she had been warned, a hard taskmaster, but she also learned that the person he drove hardest was himself. He didn't lay down the law on how he wanted things done, he just knew the result he was aiming for, and expected her to achieve it.

He directed her to the file his pregnant personal assistant had prepared before she went on leave, which explained his routine simply but clearly. She also realised very quickly that even if the only reason he had employed her was to ensure her silence, he nevertheless was in dire need of an experienced PA. Jane was a pleasant girl and eager to learn, but Helen had been right to say she needed everything spelled out to her, and having had a number of different girls from the company pool working for him before Lara arrived hadn't been conducive to the way Dominic liked his office to run — efficiently high-tech with an underlying atmosphere of calm.

'Can you design me a database?' His tone showed he expected to be disappointed.

'Of course,' she replied tartly, and was rewarded by a slight nod of reluctant approval.

For the first few days he watched her like a hawk, and their exchanges were terse, but towards the end of the second week he seemed to relax as she demonstrated those skills that had taken her to the top of her profession, and which made his life so much easier.

It was a huge job being PA to such a busy man, and once he was convinced of both her ability and her silence, he was often away from the company headquarters, leaving her to hold the fort. She looked after the mail and dealt with his emails, as well as organising his diary. He seemed to have boundless energy, attending breakfast briefings and working through to dinner engagements.

But although the work did not faze her, she found it hard to be in close proximity to Dominic every day. She could not forget his stated opinion that she was a loose canon, likely to betray Hal. It rankled that he should think she was like that when, in fact, it was so far from the values she had been brought up to believe in. Whenever she thought about it, her blood boiled, which was hardly conducive to demonstrating she was a reasonable, even-tempered woman who had no intention of making a scene!

Yet — and inexplicably in spite of that anger — she was aware that he still held a strong attraction for her, so that when she glanced up from her pad and found him looking at her intently she experienced an odd sensation and became so flustered she lost her place.

'Something wrong?' he demanded.

She shook her head mutely, and pulled her legs towards her, tucking them under her chair as if to escape him. She found it hard not to wriggle under his dark-eyed scrutiny and couldn't understand how his gaze could make her more aware of herself than had that of any other man. She seemed always to be poised in anticipation, and her hands were sticky and warm and marked the pristine pages of her pad.

Dominic noted her withdrawal and wondered why she looked so defensive. There was pathos in that defiant yet desolate expression, and he could have felt sympathy for her suggested vulnerability had he not been there before and sworn he wouldn't succumb again.

'I must have the paperwork for the meeting in Leeds on Monday by tomorrow lunchtime,' he said, more sharply than he'd intended.

'Do you want me to stay tonight?'

'What an enchanting offer,' he said with a grin, 'But I prefer to be the hunter in matters of the . . . shall we say the heart, for propriety's sake?'

He was surprised at the depth of her blush, but then, she was very fair-skinned.

'You're well aware I didn't mean anything like that! I know how late you work because I often get here in the morning and find you've completed a piece of work I only finished typing the night before. I didn't mean anything like that!' she repeated. Two red spots of colour flamed on her cheeks and she pulled herself up in her chair in indignation.

He raised his eyebrows. 'I thought you did,' he mocked, forcing his voice to sound as normal as he could. It was a very long time since a woman had left him feeling as distracted as this.

Hearing him laugh, Lara felt horribly alone.

He was being coarse and unkind and interpreting her actions by his own base beliefs. Clearly her working with him was not having the effect she had hoped for — demonstrating to him that she was in fact a morally upright, honourable person. Perhaps you had to have those values yourself to recognise them in others — and after all, Dominic moved in the same circles as Hal, so where did that leave him?

Yet in spite of everything and against her will, she remained charmed by him. The aura of authority he radiated, the probing eyes and rich voice — combined with the expensive suits and discreet cologne she had come to recognise — made an irresistible mix that stirred her senses as nothing ever had before.

'I was merely offering to finish the papers tonight.' She choked on the words. 'I should have realised that someone like you would choose to misinterpret what I said! I am a personal assistant, Mr Leigh, not a good-time girl!'

She rose unsteadily to her feet, and he felt a stab of remorse as he noted her ashen face and pinched mouth.

'I didn't suggest you were. I simply thought your zealous offer was linked to getting to know your father.'

She took a deep breath.

'I can understand why you must have thought that,' she said in a sweetly reasonable tone. 'I doubt decent women find your behaviour either attractive or acceptable, so as I offered to stay, you presumed I was not a decent woman.'

'Touche!' he murmured softly. He'd deserved that. It was hardly the most flattering thing ever said about him, but then, he had not acted well. She was so lovely he wanted to believe she was not a user, like . . . but no — he wouldn't go there . . .

'No, it's all right, we can finish it tomorrow. Don't forget, I don't have far to get home, whereas you have quite a journey.'

He lived in a glamorous flat next to his office.

'It's the reason I kept the top floor when we rented out the rest of the building,' he had explained. 'It would have been far more sensible to have the ground and first floors, but I didn't want to give up my view.'

She could understand why. She loved staring out of the office window over a misty London morning, picking out the twinkling lights of the tugs as they travelled down the Thames, churning up a white foam as they went. Matchstick people scurried about like ants as they hurried to work and the light roar of the traffic invaded the silence of her office because in spite of the triple glazing, she insisted on having a window ajar.

She couldn't imagine a more perfect place. Her father might have loved the country, but she was a Londoner, and the busy, noisy city excited and attracted her. She couldn't imagine living anywhere else.

Now I don't want to imagine working anywhere else. The thought rose unbidden as she went to get her coat. *But that's ridiculous,* she scolded herself, *I'm a temp, and I like moving around!*

She wrapped her scarf around her neck and headed for the lift. She was glad to be travelling in it alone; it gave the opportunity to inspect her face minutely without appearing vain. What was it about her features that made Dominic Leigh think she was an unprincipled woman? She peered even more closely at her reflection, but only her familiar oval face stared back. She sighed.

Why had he made that suggestive comment? Although her figure was now hidden by the straight lines of her coat, she could only suppose it was her vital statistics that had guided his opinion and was filled with a feeling of regret as she realised he was no different from the other men who had ogled her and equated a full figure with an unquenchable libido!

I had thought better of him. The words came into her head uninvited, and she frowned as she wondered why. What was it about her new boss that made her want him to be above reproach, and why was she disappointed by his reaction?

He was merely demonstrating the standards of his background, and just as she found Hal's behaviour hard to accept, so she did Dominic's. She so wanted his values to fit with hers but couldn't make them, and the truth of the matter was that Dominic was blocking her way to her father. As long as he believed her a threat, he would ensure she had no chance of meeting him.

She folded her arms tightly across her chest, as if protecting herself from the overpowering emotional rush the very thought of the man who was her current boss seemed to provoke in her. She hated this feeling of being out of control — it interfered with her ability to demonstrate her innocent credentials to Dominic — because in spite of her insistence that she was not someone who sought publicity, she knew her reaction to his physical presence suggested she was. And telling her story to the world was just what Dominic did not want her to do.

'Hello, Lara.' Helen Purvis was waiting to take the lift back up to the penthouse. 'I've got to run some personnel issues past Dominic before he goes to Leeds.' She smiled. 'How are things going?'

'Fine, thank you.' Lara nodded. 'The job's very interesting.'

It was, too, for although Dominic

might not rate her personally, he made no secret of the fact he found her an excellent PA. She also was aware that while she was very good at her job and worked very hard, part of her success at Allied Markets was down to his empowering management style. Once he knew she was capable of something, he left her to it, allowing her to achieve the required outcome in whichever way she saw fit, rather than telling her how he thought it should be done. None of her previous bosses had given her such leeway, and she blossomed under the professional trust he gave her.

Now if he would only trust her personally . . .

'Yes, I've heard good things about the work you're doing.' Helen smiled conspiratorially. 'Just between you and me — Ashley, Dominic's permanent PA, told me before she went on maternity leave that she probably won't come back. This is her second baby, you see, and I understand juggling kids and a job gets harder with each additional child. Anyway, it would leave the door open for you, and I'm sure Dominic would be delighted to keep such an efficient worker.'

I'm sure he wouldn't, thought Lara, but her heart gave a wild leap at the thought of seeing him every day after her four weeks were up.

What on earth was the matter with her? The only interest she had in Dominic was getting close to Hal — any other feelings simply got in the way.

Damn the man and his mysterious appeal!

It was very confusing, she decided as she settled down on the top deck of a red London bus. She hadn't wanted to work for him, hadn't wanted anything to do with him, yet in just two weeks she had changed her views radically.

She really enjoyed using her own initiative at work and being given a high level of responsibility, yet she hated the fact that on a personal level, Dominic clearly distrusted her. She knew the main reason she wanted his approval was because she hoped he'd take the message to Hal that it would be safe to meet her, but there was more to it than that.

The man got under her skin — but why? Surely if her limited contact with Hal had taught her one thing, it was that the values she'd learned from the Dunstans were not those of the rich and powerful. Love, loyalty and kindness all meant a great deal to her, whereas they clearly didn't to Dominic. So why was she beating herself up over what he thought of her?

She pulled off a glove to pay her fare, and her mind sped back to the wedding, to the clinical chill of the registry office, the welcoming warmth of Wyscom Old Hall and the delicious sensations when she'd danced with Dominic . . .

She gave an involuntary gasp, and balled her hands into fists, the pale pink nails of her bare right hand biting into the flesh of her palm. Embarrassed, she used her gloved left hand to wipe the condensation from the steamed up window beside her. She stared out sightlessly at the busy London rush hour. Normally the hurry and bustle excited her, but today she was too deep in thought even to register the scene.

She didn't understand what was happening to her. How could she be so physically drawn to a man whose moral outlook she loathed? She could not deny what she felt when around him, and despised herself for it, yet was powerless to resist. She felt vaguely ashamed of her emotions, and that she seemed powerless to stop them.

She remembered Nanny Blore's pronouncement about her mother at Henrietta's wedding, and wondered if it was true what she'd said about Chloe and whether she had inherited the same.

Yet she kept going back to the fact that she had not felt this way about other men, and surely if she were simply focused on pleasure, she would not have been so selective. And Henrietta had told her that Nanny Bore disliked Hal's second wife for replacing the first, so who was to say her opinion was a valid one? Indeed, her sister had told her she doubted whether their mother could have lived knowing Hal was with another woman in spite of their divorce — what were the words she had used? Something about not playing second fiddle and Hal being the love of her life.

By the time she reached home it was dark, and she turned on the log effect gas fire in the lounge and curled up in a comfy armchair.

Against all expectation she was enjoying working with Dominic, and she was pleased she had earned his respect as his PA. But she wanted him to respect her as a person as well. His ill-concealed contempt for what he believed to be her riotous lifestyle when she was in fact living like a nun, was not only hurtful, but more importantly, was scuppering her plans to gain access to

Hal. Dominic's good opinion of her was important for that plan, but even if it hadn't been, she didn't like him thinking she was just someone on the make, who would sell her story at the drop of a hat. But he seemed fixed in his belief.

I'll just have to accept it, she thought, but she didn't underestimate how difficult that would be.

7

'Lara, would you please email me the financial strategy for our new Larant enterprise?'

Dominic's mellow tones filled the office as he spoke on the phone. Lara had turned on her telephone microphone the previous week, when he had called to ask her to look for some papers in his office and she had needed to be able to work away from the receiver under his instructions of where to search. Having discovered how soothing she found his rich dark tones surrounding her, she now left the mechanism on whenever he was away from the office.

'Will do. How are things going?'

'Pretty well.' his voice crackled over the primitive telecommunications system that was considered one of the better ones in eastern Eurasia. She could hear he sounded pleased, if cautious. 'They like what we're suggesting and see that we could work together, but it's not in the bag yet. They want to come to England and have a look around, see how we do things and whether we can actually deliver. I may have to stay a few days to get everything sorted.'

Lara's heart sank at the news. She knew it meant there was less chance for her to work on him to arrange a meeting with Hal — but surely, even allowing for that, her reaction was a bit extreme? Dominic had been away for four days now, and she was surprised that she actually missed him. Even her wonderful view had palled with the knowledge there was no chance of him coming into her office and sharing it with her.

'Don't forget that Hal is due to be confirmed in post next weekend,' she said, and then could have bitten off her tongue. She had grasped at the one thing she thought could convince him to come back before she left his employment, thus giving her a final chance to achieve her dream — but in doing so, she had broken her strict rule not to mention her father.

An uneasy truce had grown between them and professionally their relationship was very proper, but any mention of Hal Lawrence and Dominic withdrew into a cold, forbidding shell. Not that Lara wanted to discuss her father until Dominic was prepared to introduce them — but Hal was a famous man, and due to his imminent rise to power, was often forced upon them via the daily papers or newscasts. When that happened Dominic would look sideways at her across the room with his mouth set in a hard line and his brows knitted, and she always felt snubbed and at a disadvantage. Sometimes she would catch him watching her when he didn't think she was looking, and she was furious with herself for always giving a start and averting her eyes guiltily. What was he observing her for, and why did she jump as if she had done something wrong?

'Going out tonight?' he had asked after just one such occasion,

'What? Oh, no, I'm going home.' She was flustered by his question, surprised that he should care what she was doing.

'You had that distant look of love's young dream,' he said. 'I thought perhaps you were meeting a boyfriend.'

She dropped her eyes and leaned down to make a show of getting something from her desk drawer so he shouldn't see her blushing. It was perceptive of him, she thought, because she had indeed been thinking about a man — but one who seemed completely indifferent to her.

'Do you have a boyfriend?' he demanded as if he had a right to know. He seemed strangely tense, and a pulse throbbed in his temple.

Lara suppressed a facetious desire to say 'Hundreds!' She wished she could claim a list of eager suitors, but it didn't occur to her to lie.

'I'm between boyfriends for now,' she

said, and even to her it sounded odd.

'Changeable affections, eh?' He curled his lip. 'I suppose you like to keep yourself available in case a better prospect comes along.'

'What?' Her inflection demonstrated her puzzlement. 'I just don't happen to have met anyone I want to go out with at the moment.'

He regarded her coldly. 'Was that why you made such an exhibition of yourself dancing at the wedding? Looking for a new beau?'

'Hardly!' Lara pooh-poohed his suggestion. 'I'm not that keen on Hooray Henrys.' But she was confused. What on earth had made him think that? Whatever it was, she could see his interpretation of what had happened was going to be a stumbling block between them — however hard she tried to gain his approval for her circumspection in her private life, he would recall his interpretation of the way she had behaved.

Yet it hadn't been so very terrible

— her enthusiasm could have been seen as embarrassing maybe, but not a hanging offence! She saw she was going to have to address the problem if there was to be any hope of him changing his opinion about her and passing the word onto Hal. Actually, she wanted to say a very rude word, but he was her boss, after all, so she settled for an air of haughty superiority.

'As you wish.' His tone made it plain he didn't believe her.

* * *

Dominic had watched her fetch her coat and nodded when she bade him goodnight. He was annoyed by the way he'd felt it necessary to pry into her affairs, but seeing her sitting there, so inviting, he hadn't wanted her to go. The thought of her leaving him to meet another man bothered him, and he'd wanted the reassurance of her denial that there wasn't anyone special.

He hadn't got it, though. The idea

that such a beautiful young woman was going to spend Friday night alone was ridiculous, and her assertion that she was had only served to convince him anew that he had been correct in his belief that she wasn't to be trusted. She wouldn't recognise the truth if it hit her in the face!

The trouble was, annoyed though he had been at the time, now when he remembered her fluid movements in the glittering lights on the dance floor, he wished she'd been dancing for him.

He'd been a fool to employ her. Oh, she was good at her job — no, to be fair, she was excellent — but he was irked by his inability to ignore the strong attraction he felt for her. She was a lovely woman, and he didn't need that edge of tension that now pervaded the office.

Still, it was only a couple of weeks until the business with Hal would be complete, and then he could get rid of her. He was surprised at how depressed that made him feel.

He recalled that feeling now, as she reminded him of the approaching date, but he refused to show it.

'Indeed,' he said disdainfully, 'I'm sure we both have the date ringed on our calendars, me because Hal will then be beyond your reach, and you because you'll gain your freedom.'

★   ★   ★

Dominic's expressive voice left Lara in no doubt that he was counting the days until she left. She felt a kick of disappointment as she heard his words, and reasoned she was so upset because he obviously still thought her a threat to her father.

Why, oh, why had she mentioned Hal — and just when they seemed to be getting on better? Anyway, he'd made no secret of the fact that he was longing to see the back of her, and she was simply going to have to get used to it.

Thinking of Hal reminded her that Henrietta and Gareth were back from their honeymoon, so she rang her sister's mobile to ask how she was.

'Oh, hi, Lara!' Henrietta was as bouncy as usual. 'We had a fabulous time — lots of sun and sand and sangria! I can thoroughly recommend married life.'

'I'm glad you had a good time.'

'I know — Gareth is out at a lodge meeting tonight. Why don't you come over and see our new flat and we can order a pizza and catch up?'

* * *

At six o'clock, Lara walked up to the elegant Victorian building just off Sloane Square where Hal had bought his daughter and her husband a flat as their wedding present. She gave a wry smile as she acknowledged her sister probably fitted the description of what used to be called a Sloane Ranger, those fashionable and upper-class young ladies living the conventional social life of people from their background, and she idly wondered where she fitted in. Not at all, in spite of her shared parentage.

She entered the foyer and was momentarily taken aback as she registered that the interior was designed in the most contemporary of styles, and she realised that only the façade of the original old building remained. She was barely inside the door before the concierge was bearing down upon her, wanting to know her business.

'I've come to see Mrs Poole,' Lara explained, remembering to use her sister's married name, and was amused by the immediate change in his attitude. He confirmed with Henrietta by phone that Lara was expected, and then directed her to the correct lift and floor.

Henrietta was waiting by her door, tanned and relaxed, ushered Lara inside, and flung her arms around her sister and gave her a hug.

'It's great to see you!' She enthused. 'I've been stuck here all week waiting for furniture and fittings to be delivered, so I feel quite cut off.'

'You mean you haven't even been out to the shops?' Lara teased. She knew Henrietta was an inveterate shopper, and had noted the boutiques and famous fashion names she had passed on her way to the flat.

Henrietta laughed. 'Well, perhaps I have just popped into Harvey Nicks,' she admitted, using the affectionate nickname that was applied to that most dignified of stores, 'and Harrods is only a short stroll. Isn't it heaven, living only doors away? I must have spent a fortune over the past week.'

If the contents of the flat were anything to go by, she certainly had, Lara thought. Unapologetically modern, the rich and welcoming interior boasted enough equipment and appliances to stock a small shop, and the overall impression was one of luxury and prestige. Proudly her sister showed her round the four-bed duplex, before taking her to the window and pointing to Hyde Park.

'So,' she said when they were sitting down with glasses of wine, 'what have you been doing?'

'Not a lot.' Lara smiled. 'You know I've been working for Dominic Leigh — '

'What?' Henrietta was all ears. 'Working for old Dom the Bomb? How did that come about?'

So Hal hadn't told Henrietta of his plan to keep Lara under control until after his post was announced by arranging for her to work for Dominic? Well, she wouldn't spill the beans.

'You know I'm junior partner in a temping agency?' Lara decided not to labour the point. 'Well, Dominic approached us to see if we had a senior PA available. It just happened I was free — pure chance, really.'

'Pooh!' Henrietta snorted. 'Dominic never leaves anything to chance. If he got you as his secretary it was because he wanted you, and he will have arranged everything down to the last detail to ensure he did.'

'What makes you say that?'

Henrietta sighed. 'Well, you must admit, he is rather gorgeous, and I used to have the hots for him.' She did not mince her words. 'Sadly, he wasn't in the least bit interested, but I think he felt I was rather out of his class.'

She excused his rejection with the self-confidence only the daughter of inherited wealth and position could bring to bear.

'How do you mean?' Lara was confused. 'Dominic is rich and comes from the same background, doesn't he?'

Henrietta pulled a face. 'Rich, yes, but he's not one of us,' she said without a thought for Lara nor a trace of embarrassment. 'He's a self-made man. His father ran a small haulage firm, I believe, and it was about to go bankrupt when Dom took it over. He turned the company round, and hasn't looked back since.'

Lara digested this news in silence. So he didn't come from the same world as Hal and his cronies . . . in which case, why was he supporting them? For, while Henrietta might not be aware of it, her sister was quite sure Dominic had employed her at their father's behest. Why else would he bring someone he clearly disliked so closely into his life?

'I didn't know that,' was all she said. 'Why do you call him Dom the Bomb?'

'Oh, you know.' Henrietta raised her eyes heavenwards. 'He's so upstanding and moral and bossy, and if anyone dares to do anything he deems reprehensible he explodes like dynamite. There was some woman who behaved abominably to him years ago, and apparently he exploded, so she gave him the nickname, and it's stuck.'

'Do you know her name?' Lara tried to sound nonchalant, but Henrietta wasn't fooled.

'Why? You haven't fallen for him, have you?' she probed. 'Be careful, Lara. He's like Pa, strictly a safety-in-numbers sort of guy. Definitely not the marrying kind.'

Lara shifted uncomfortably. What a ridiculous thing for Henrietta to say. Of course she wasn't thinking about marriage! She'd told Malcolm she was her own woman and lived alone now.

Remembering her two-up-two-down cottage, she couldn't help comparing it to Henrietta's new pad. The Dunstans had modernised to a degree, but their house retained many original features, and did not pretend to be what it was not. It remained an artisan's cottage, and Lara was glad of it. This sumptuous apartment with its state-of-the-art air conditioning, audio-visual equipment and smart technology did not tempt her. She could see it suited Henrietta's lifestyle, but it wouldn't have suited hers.

After they had eaten their pizzas and Henrietta had given her reluctant sister a blow-by-blow account of her honeymoon, Lara tried again to learn more about Dominic's mysterious woman.

'Really, I don't know much about it,' admitted Henrietta. She had drunk rather a lot of wine and was stumbling over her words. 'It was in the early days, and I think they were unofficially engaged. Anyway, he trusted her absolutely — that shows you how long ago it must have been! — and his company was putting in a very important bid for a rival firm. She didn't work for him or anything like that, but there must have been a certain amount of pillow talk, because next thing he knows, she's blabbed to the opposition, and the whole deal went down the pan and he nearly lost his business! Then she left him for the chairman of the other company, and he's never allowed a woman get close to him since. He doesn't trust us, you see. Steer well clear, Lara,' she warned, 'He's not called Dom the Bomb for nothing!'

★　★　★

On the Tube on the way home, Lara mulled over what she had been told.

As the carriage rocked and creaked between stations, she wondered what Dominic's ex-fiancé had been like; the girl he had loved enough to want to marry, and who had let him down. She understood now why he had doubted her — he'd been taken in once before by a woman who had used her body to bridge his defences, so it was no wonder he believed she had also been acting. But it was so unfair that because one woman had lied and cheated, her whole gender should be tarred with the same brush, and she found herself getting angry with someone she didn't even know.

This is ridiculous! she thought, but the feelings wouldn't go. Perhaps she could use this knowledge to overcome Dominic's aversion to her, though she couldn't at the moment see how. Nevertheless, her spirits were lighter than they had been when she had set out that evening, and while his past experience did not excuse his behaviour to her — because she felt he had been rude and unkind — it did go some way to explaining why he had acted as he did.

There was a light fog as she walked home from the station, but she was so deep in thought she hardly noticed. As she rounded the corner into her road, she caught sight of a car just driving away from outside her house, and for one moment had a feeling she knew it, but it passed as quickly as it had come.

I'm just on edge and imagining things, she thought, and looked forward to a good night's sleep. She had been lying awake until late for the past few days, wishing her situation were different and powerless to make it so. Now that she understood it wasn't so much her as women in general that Dominic distrusted she felt a great deal better, and sure enough, shortly after her head hit the pillow, she drifted off into a reinvigorating and dreamless sleep.

★   ★   ★

Lara was glad of this the next day, when Dominic phoned her early and rapped out a long set of instructions he wanted dealt with at once.

'Paul Osten and his wife Maria are coming back to England with me tomorrow,' he explained, 'and I need you to make all the arrangements.'

He must have made a good impression to be on first name terms with the director of the newly privatised distribution company of the previously hard-line east European state he was visiting, she thought, and listened carefully as he listed his requirements.

'I want you to book them into a good hotel — comfortable, but not too ostentatious. Paul still finds the transition from collectivism to capitalism rather hard to take,' he said, 'but his wife is keen to become accustomed to a more comfortable life.' He chuckled. 'Maria will want to go shopping and sight-seeing, and I want you to make all the arrangements and accompany her. Jane can earn her pay as your assistant while the Ostens are here. Maria speaks pretty good English, and is good fun.' Again he laughed, and Lara thought how relaxed he sounded. 'Also, I need you to contact the Home Office and arrange bank accounts for overseas workers and contact our industrial services manager and work with him to prepare papers and the logistics involved with housing, lease ends and movement of staff to new contracts. Think you can do that?'

'Yes.' She didn't doubt herself. She knew she was good at what she did and was pleased for the opportunity to demonstrate her skills to Dominic. She wasn't sure how much she would enjoy acting as nursemaid to an east European wannabe princess, but if it was what she was being paid to do, she would do it to the best of her ability.

She whizzed through Dominic's emails and the complex diary management that working at her level in such a high-powered company required, before making the necessary phone calls to the business unit managers to explain Dominic's wishes. She was gratified by the feedback she was receiving from these senior managers, which indicated their appreciation of her reliability, integrity and ability. Perhaps they'd feed that back to Dominic and influence his opinion of her.

Once she had managed the business to her satisfaction, she began searching for a suitable hotel for the Ostens, but whereas she would normally have used her contacts and knowledge from previous jobs to inform her final decision, on this occasion it was something much more fey which led her to make the booking. Skimming the directory, her eyes focused on the name Wyscom Hotel, and she had immediately been drawn to the unusually-named hostelry.

It turned out to be a small, exclusive establishment in a quiet but central position, ideally placed for both Markets House and the West End. Prices were no less exclusive, but Dominic had made it clear he wanted his guests to feel cosseted without pretension, and this family-run business seemed to fit the bill. She visited the hotel to make sure all was in order, before booking a suite for the European couple.

She arranged for a limousine to collect the travellers from Heathrow, and having given Jane clear instructions on how she was to manage the office over the next few days, was at the hotel to greet them. She told herself that by being part of the welcoming committee she was merely demonstrating those hospitality skills for which Dominic paid her, but she couldn't get away from a nagging feeling that it was her own need to see that singular, separate man as soon as possible that had guided her itinerary.

Dominic stepped out of the car first. With one quick movement he was standing on the pavement, watching to see the chauffeur help Mrs Osten from the car, before turning and acknowledging Lara's presence.

He surveyed her with a critical expression. She was warmly dressed in a fake fur coat and long boots, but she was aware it was not the cold that was making her skin tingle with goose bumps. His dark hair needed a trim — he had told her he didn't trust foreign barbers and she had made an appointment for him with his regular hairdresser later that day — but the extra curl flopping over his forehead simply added to his devastating good looks by accentuating a certain boyishness. Indeed, he was looking remarkably stress-free for someone who had spent the last week racing around a former totalitarian state that was struggling for independent survival. Lara was aware that Chekurov had some way to go before its business community could be considered a model of good practice, and was surprised at how laid-back her boss appeared to be about it.

'They are good people,' he told her later when they had settled the couple at their hotel and returned to the office to catch up with urgent work. 'Not obsessed by anyone's station in life, but focusing on their ability to make things better. Paul is truly committed to the cause of improving the lot of his countrymen and sees that having a thriving business community is the way to achieve it.' His eyes were shining as he spoke. 'Now do you see why it is so important we have someone like Hal working for the future of our country, both here and with our European allies?'

Lara nodded, surprised he should be lauding a classless society when she had thought he applauded her father's unearned privileges, and unsure how he would turn if she started talking about Hal.

'You've done well.' He went over the work she had done in his absence. 'I know I'm high-maintenance and demanding as a boss, and I need someone who is able to pick things up and run with them when I'm not here.'

He paused and she basked in his praise. She had come to realise his approbation meant a great deal to her.

'I'm quite bossy and very systems-led.' Lara played down all she had done, mindful of Mrs Dunstan's frequent exhortations not to show off. 'So I tend to organise people at work. But you're a clear thinker who knows exactly what he wants, so you make my job quite easy.'

'Let's hope you still think so by the time the Ostens have left,' he said with a grin. 'You'll be working hard over the next few days, not only over-seeing your normal office work with Jane, but also shepherding Mrs Osten about.'

* * *

In fact it proved no hardship, because Maria Osten was the easiest person to like. Short and dumpy in too-tight, ill-chosen clothes, she fell in love with London and everyone in it. She adored the Houses of Parliament, the Tower of London, and Horse Guards Parade, snuggled down under a blanket on a boat trip down the River Thames, happily correcting the commentator from the guide book on her knee if she felt he had left anything out. She shrieked her appreciation at the top of the London Eye, and made considerable inroads into mountains of fast food which she explained were not yet available in her country.

As they hurried around the capital's tourist traps, Lara sometimes got the oddest feeling that they were being watched — but who would be in the least bit interested in them? She couldn't imagine, dismissing ideas of secret service agents and spying as quickly as they arose. The Cold War was over, after all. In fact, when she analysed it, she realised what was happening. Maria was so full of life, and with her unusual dress sense and infectious laughter, everyone turned to marvel at her. It was obviously this that was causing the uncomfortable prickling at the back of her neck — but even knowing that, she was surprised to note it wouldn't go away.

Maria's real passion was shopping. Shoes, dresses, coats, underwear, hats; there was no piece of women's apparel she did not try on with the same lack of judgment she applied to everything she saw. It was all, 'Vunderfool, Lar-rr-a, vunderfool!'

So it was that when she and her husband invited Dominic to dinner at their hotel, and having insisted Lara should come too, that Mrs Osten waddled out to greet them in a shocking pink confection of frills and bows which accentuated her every extra ounce, and gave her the appearance of a particularly overdressed plastic doll.

Yet he loves her completely! Lara marvelled, as she saw the delighted and proprietary look Paul Osten gave his wife. How wonderful, to be cherished so fondly that no matter what one did, one was seen as perfect.

'Paul and I met when we were very young,' Maria confided. 'Too young, but we could not wait. We had to be together, but in pre-independent Chekurov, if you were not married . . . ' She gave an expressive shrug, and shook her head.

'What did you do?'

Paul Osten laughed. 'Like most young people in love, we ducked and dived, finding privacy where we could. But then Maria became pregnant, and that was a problem.'

Lara felt herself stiffen. Why was it that babies conceived out of wedlock through no fault of their own — babies like her — were always seen as a nuisance? Was she about to hear another tale of an abandoned love child?

'Why?'

'Because I lost my role in the Party for immorality, and that meant I had no chance to influence the changes I felt the country needed for many years.'

Maria squeezed her husband's hand.

'He sacrificed everything for me and Carola, our daughter,' she explained proudly.

'But what about the important work you were doing?' Dominic asked.

'Nothing is more important than my family,' Paul said simply. 'What kind of person would I have been if I had devoted myself to suffering humanity, all while ignoring the needs of those I loved?'

Lara flashed him a smile of approval and noted that Dominic was deep in thought.

'Children matter,' she said quietly, and saw those shaded dark eyes watching her from under hooded lids as she finished her soup.

I could drown in those eyes! she thought, and then pulled herself up short. She'd been coming up with some strange ideas recently and wasn't sure she liked where they were taking her. Because of that she had resolutely refused to examine her feelings too closely, subconsciously recognising that to do so might take her to a place best not to go. She must concentrate on her goal, which was to meet Hal and be accepted by him.

But it seemed that Dominic was the doorman. She needed to gain his approval before he'd let her near her father, so she must act like one of those coolly restrained upper crust women he seemed to admire so much and not as a passionate hot-head.

Lara wasn't helped in her resolve when Dominic insisted on driving her home. When the car rolled silently to a stop outside her house, she made to get out, but he leaned across the gear stick and caught her hand.

'Why so keen to run off?' he asked in a low, modulated voice. 'We still have to discuss plans for Friday.'

'Friday?' The day her contract with Allied Markets came to an end. Her spirits rose — he was going to ask her to stay on!

'Yes, I want to return the hospitality and take Maria and Paul out somewhere swish for the evening,' he explained. 'Where would you suggest?'

Lara had to fight the dark cloud of disappointment that descended on her. How stupid she'd been to imagine he'd want to extend her employment. Hadn't his behaviour demonstrated he only suffered her presence to ensure Hal's safe election? She had to force herself to consider his question about entertaining.

'Actually, if you want to build rapport with the Ostens, I think they'd prefer to be invited to your apartment,' she said. 'Maria is a real home bird, and although she's enjoying being pampered, you saw for yourself tonight how much store they set on family life.'

He looked surprised. 'But I don't have a 'family life', as you put it. And I can't cook.'

'You don't have to.' She laughed in spite of her gloom. 'It's not so much about having a wife and children galloping about the place, more a demonstration that you respect Paul and Maria enough to allow them to share something of your personal life. Building up trust takes more than a sober professional relationship.'

He thought for a moment, then said, 'You're right. It's not as if Paul and I will get the opportunity to meet regularly at those other important business settings which cement commercial activities, the golf course or gentlemen's club.'

'Ah, yes — golf.' She laughed again. 'From what Maria has told me about Paul and exercise, I rather think he'd agree with the person who said golf was a good walk spoiled!'

'Mark Twain.' He filled in the name. 'You seem to have learned a lot about the Ostens in the short time they've been here. Maria has really taken to you. OK, we'll have them to dinner.'

'We?' She couldn't have heard right.

'Of course.' He gave a lazy shrug. 'Where else can I get a hostess at such short notice? And I know your table manners pass muster, don't I?'

She bit her lip. The wedding, of course.

'I'll arrange the catering and make all the arrangements.' She went into her busy personal assistant mode to cover her embarrassment.

'OK, Miss Efficiency.' He grinned. 'I'll leave it all to you.'

She leaned down to pick up her handbag from the footwell and as she sat up, saw he was staring ahead, body tensed and brow creased.

His eyes narrowed. 'You see that car up there — parked where the road turns — do you know it?'

She peered where he was pointing, but the silver saloon looked much like any other in the shadows, and she shook her head.

'There's someone in it,' he said, 'and I thought he was looking this way.'

'It's not a someone, it's a some two.' Lara giggled as another head came into view in the passenger seat. 'And I should imagine they have much better things to do than watch us!'

'Hmm.' Dominic's shoulders relaxed slightly, but she could tell he was still on edge.

'See you tomorrow,' she said reluctantly, wishing she had the nerve to invite him in but knowing she would get a negative response. 'Maria and I are going to Lambeth Palace first thing, so I won't be in until about one o'clock.'

He shook his head. 'You won't see me at all,' he said. 'I'm taking Paul to inspect some of the warehouses we've set up in the Home Counties and won't be back until Friday night. I'm going to have to leave everything to you, OK?'

'OK.' She nodded, and turned to walk up the garden path.

★ ★ ★

The next day Lara and Maria caught a taxi to the south bank of the Thames and joined the queue of expectant visitors lined up outside the entrance to the building which had been the home of the Archbishops of Canterbury since the twelfth century. Maria liked palaces that were still occupied by the intended original inhabitants, be they princes or prelates, both species having disappeared long ago from her country.

As they stood in line, the two of them chatted easily. It was true what Dominic had said, Lara thought, she and the bouncy, indefatigable east European had really hit it off.

Maria did not sit on ceremony in spite of the fact that she was well aware Lara was Dominic's employee, and as such, paid to be at her beck and call. But that was not her way, and Lara had soon felt like an old friend. So she wasn't surprised when she was quizzed about her relationship with Dominic.

'He is very handsome, that one!' Mrs Osten gave a wink. 'You two are an item?' Her English had in part been gleaned from American movies and was very idiosyncratic.

'Oh, no, not at all!' Lara answered too quickly, determined not to be seen as the boss's perk.

'But he likes you. I know. I see how he watches you when you are not looking. He would like more, I think.'

'You must be joking!' Lara couldn't stop herself. 'He accepts I'm a good secretary, but our private lives are miles apart.'

'For now, maybe,' the older woman said with a smug smile. 'But I am never wrong, so one day I will tell you 'I told you so'.'

Lara considered this as they sat through the video commentary that opened their visit to Lambeth Palace.

She had to admit that Maria's words had made her heart leap, even while she knew the older woman was wrong. But why should it?

She knew Dominic only wanted her around so he could keep her away from Hal until after he was safely in post. And she stayed so that she could eventually meet her father properly. It was a no brainer.

But if that really was the only reason

she stuck around, why, when she thought about leaving Allied Markets, did she get not so much a going-to-the-dentist feeling, as a condemned-cell one?

She gasped. A thought had leaped into her mind of such ridiculous proportions that it left her quite breathless. Her stomach gave a sickening lurch, but even as it did so, an aura of peace descended over her racing mental mapping.

Suddenly it all fell into place and she knew why she was feeling so disjointed and out of control.

She had fallen in love with Dominic Leigh!

8

Once Lara realised that fact, it was so simple, really. She was just like her mother — but not in the way Nanny Blore had described at the wedding, rather as Henrietta had reported she had been told when she grew up.

Chloe had been a one-man woman who had loved deeply and refused to contemplate sharing, and Lara recognised a kindred spirit. Malcolm had been wrong — she wasn't cold — the reason she hadn't been attracted in the same way to other boyfriends was because she didn't feel deeply for them and didn't care if they saw other women.

With Dominic it was different. Every moment she was in his company, she was aware of him. That was why she was so distressed that he had such a low opinion of her as a person — she wanted him to rate her.

Love — what a tiny word to embrace such a huge emotion! It transcended animal instinct and turned it into something eternal and true. She relived the deep, disturbing, delightful feelings she experienced when Dominic was around, and for one scary, amazing moment allowed herself the luxury of imagining him feeling the same way.

She closed her eyes and sighed as she heard him say, 'I love you, Lara'. Then reality clicked in.

'Fat chance!' She spat the words out with such venom that Maria blinked in surprise.

'Excuse me?'

'Oh, I just remembered something I should have done,' Lara ad-libbed to hide her outburst, and her companion nodded and returned her attention to the video.

However, Lara found it impossible to concentrate on anything but her momentous discovery. The trouble was, Dominic had made it abundantly clear that whereas she made a good personal assistant, the idea that she might assist in other areas of his life was quite ludicrous.

He might not have had the same background as Hal, but he obviously admired that behaviour, and wouldn't consider someone as lowly as she for a date. He seemed to hanker after the lifestyle her father enjoyed, displaying little spontaneity and weighing up the outcome of everything before taking action.

She realised it was going to be very hard working so closely with him and yet keeping her distance now that she knew she loved him.

★ ★ ★

Lara spent all of Friday preparing for the dinner party. Fortunately, she had already booked for the indomitable Maria to have a pampering day at a health club, so she was able to plough straight into making the arrangements for the evening.

First she needed to see the flat. Dominic had left his keys on her desk with a note:

Won't be back until six. Feel free to rearrange everything as you see fit — I trust your judgment.

Four words leaped out at her from his message. *I trust your judgment.* She knew he was referring to her business sense, but it gave her a tiny spark of hope.

If he had learned to trust her integrity as a professional, surely she could convince him that not all women were faithless and disloyal? Well, she could try, she supposed, but there was something about Dominic's forbidding expression when he mentioned relationships that made her doubt it. Presumably he favoured Hal's upper crust example of safety in numbers and was not looking for permanence. It was just her hard luck that not only was she not out of the top drawer — or maybe she was, since Hal was her father, after all — her values meant

she'd never consider a casual relationship.

She looked out over the city below
and thought how lucky it was that she
and Maria were not out sightseeing
today. The sky was a dark gun metal
grey. Watching the television weather
forecast before she had left for work,
Lara had noted the surprise with which
the diminutive announcer stated snow
was on the way. It was certainly
unseasonably cold, and the late Indian
summer that had lingered through early
autumn was now no more than a
distant memory.

She contacted a catering company
she had used before to supply directors'
lunches and discussed the type of food
they would serve. She was torn between
wanting to create a homely atmosphere,
which she had recognised was what
Maria loved best and was missing, and
a more formal presentation to impress
her husband. Domesticity won, for Lara
acknowledged that Paul put such a high
value on his wife's opinion, it was more

important to ensure she had had a good time than to appear sophisticated.

Before she ordered the flowers, she needed to see the flat and get a feel for what would go best, so she walked out across the hall to Dominic's front door. She unlocked it and then paused on the threshold, feeling vaguely guilty about entering his home when he was not there.

Don't be daft, she chided herself, *he's hardly going to have left a booby trap for you!*

She strode purposefully into the room.

It was a large L-shaped room with an outer wall of glass, giving a panoramic view of London untrammelled by curtains. She stood for a moment looking out at the Palace of Westminster and the Thames as it flowed down towards the City of London, and then turned her attention to the apartment itself.

The overall impression was one of light, space and scale. The pale hardwood floor complemented the off-white walls, and although the furniture consisted of large, modern pieces, they fitted easily into the vast open plan expanse. By far the most imposing feature was the fireplace, all steel and glass and suspended from the ceiling in the centre of the room. Beneath and surrounding it; the only floor covering in the apartment was a large patchwork rug of shaggy white sheepskin.

Lara could not decide whether she liked the flat or not. It was certainly very elegant and smacked of good taste, but it didn't really look lived-in. There were no photos or books or knick-knacks, all of which to her made a house a home. It was as if the person who lived here had no character of his own. And that was odd, because Dominic clearly did have strong opinions, but his flat didn't reflect a personality at all.

There were a number of good prints strategically placed around the walls, and she recognised the largest as a copy of Magritte's *Les Amants*. She liked surrealist painters but had always found the draped faces of the two lovers in this one, hidden and mysterious as they were, rather disquieting. It wasn't what she would have chosen for pride of place in her home.

The kitchen was similarly sleek, the stainless steel doors, worktops and equipment giving it a professional look that the colossal island cooker did nothing to dispel. She smiled wryly as she inspected the two massive ovens, frying plate and gas burners. The magnificent machine could provide every possible permutation of cooking, which was rather a waste, really, considering all it was going to be required to do was to keep ready-prepared food warm until it was served.

She opened the cupboards to check on utensils and found an exquisite white Japanese dinner service that looked as if it had never been used, and a canteen of beautifully crafted stainless steel cutlery.

No wonder Dominic had been so surprised at her suggestion that he should invite the Ostens to his flat — it didn't appear he ever entertained at home at all.

Two drawers of fine linen gave her a good choice from which to dress the table, but there were no personal touches. It looked to her as if a designer had created what he considered to be an award-winning contemporary apartment, expecting his client to add the finishing touches to make it his own — only the client hadn't.

She wondered where Dominic usually ate or kept his clutter. She supposed he could be one of those people who liked his living space to be kept clear and to do so put more personal items in the bedrooms, but she didn't dream of putting this theory to the test. She still felt something of a trespasser on his territory just being in his kitchen, and was glad to leave once she had laid the table and set the fire.

She returned later when the flowers arrived.

'Why, this is just stunning!' the florist whistled as she took him in. 'Where do you want these?'

'The table decoration over there, and then I thought a tall arrangement by the window, and the red roses here, next to this two-seater sofa.'

'Romantic evening, is it?' he smiled.

'No!' she replied unnecessarily sharply and saw him flinch. 'At least, not for me,' she smiled, trying to make amends and actually making things worse.

'Don't you worry, love.' He gave her a comforting smile. 'With these flowers and your looks he won't stand a chance!'

She didn't try to explain, and simply let him put the finishing touches to the arrangements.

She had chosen the red roses as a tribute to the love Paul and Maria clearly had for one another and knew

Maria would be delighted with them. The trouble was, she acknowledged, as the crimson blossoms were so closely associated with romance, it was possible Dominic would construe her choice as being aimed at him, and that would be a disaster! He already believed she was trying to get close to him for her own ends — what if he saw her as giving him a message via the language of flowers?

What the heck, she shrugged, it was too late to worry about that now. She would only just have time to dash home and change before she'd have to be back to greet the visitors with Dominic.

★ ★ ★

When she got home she felt strangely elated and collapsed on a stool in the tiny kitchen with a cup of tea while she waited for her bath to run. She heard a commotion in the back garden and saw her neighbour's cat about to pounce on something in her flowerbed.

'Shoo!' she yelled out of the back door and chased the tabby back over the fence. It was too cold to stay outside for long, and she turned quickly to return indoors, but as she did so, a flash of light caught her eyes from the upstairs window of one of the terraced houses whose gardens backed onto hers. She looked up, startled, but apart from the half-pulled curtain, she saw nothing. A trick of the light, she thought, and hurried back into the warmth of the kitchen.

She dressed with great care that evening and tried to convince herself it had nothing to do with Dominic. Her wardrobe was not extensive, but she had learned the trick of paying for a small number of good quality clothes that lasted well rather than a mountain of cheaper ones. She cast a critical eye over all her evening wear and chose a black sheath dress with a short sequined jacket, which emphasised her figure and gave dramatic contrast to her creamy, pale complexion. She caught her blonde hair into a knot on top of her head, and round her neck she wore the row of pearls that had been an eighteenth birthday present from the Dunstans.

She decided she looked OK, and content that there was no more she could do, was about to pull on a warm coat before running for the bus, when her doorbell rang.

'Are you ready? I thought it easier if I collected you.' Dominic was on the doorstep, looking a million dollars in an expensive grey charcoal suit.

'I should've put on my coat,' she said, as he helped her into the warm interior of his car.

'No need,' he said. 'I'll be bringing you home, and you won't have time to get cold in the short dash from the pavement to your front door.'

She said no more, recognising the stress of rush hour driving, remaining silent for the journey.

'You've decorated the apartment well,' he said as they neared the underground car park beneath Markets House. 'Did you get a professional in or do it yourself?'

'I designed it, others did it.' Lara was pleased he hadn't commented on the floral arrangements.

Indeed, why should he? He didn't know how she felt about him, so why had she imagined he would interpret her action as declaring her love for him? He thought she wanted to get close to him to reach her father, not have a deep and meaningful relationship.

But she didn't, and she did.

★ ★ ★

Dominic led the way to the basement lift that took them all the way up to his apartment, and when they entered the flat he noted with approval that the fire he had lit just before he went out had taken hold. He had been pleasantly surprised when he first got home to see how welcoming the place looked, and now the flames were sending licking shadows of apricot and orange up the pale walls, adding warmth and comfort to what, he had to admit, was usually a fairly cold, sterile room.

He watched Lara as she busied about ensuring all was well and found himself admiring the quiet confidence with which she undertook her tasks. She had . . . what? Class and poise and serenity, and that certain indefinable something that made a woman a lady. And by that, he meant more than simply being a member of the aristocracy like Hal. It was actually about integrity and true values.

The thought surprised him. He had grown so used to seeing Lara as a girl with an agenda, it was hard to realign his opinion to the person he had come to know over the past four weeks. For while working with him she hadn't put a foot out of line. She'd had the senior managers eating out of her hand, managed the office with a professionalism beyond reproach, and refrained from trying to trick or bribe him into introducing her to Hal. He had always been suspicious about what she wanted from Hal, particularly as she had appeared on the scene at such an inopportune moment. He'd doubted her motives were genuine, but now that he knew her, he was almost sure they were.

And, he realised, he was pleased about that.

★   ★   ★

The Ostens arrived just slightly late and were clearly flattered and pleased to be invited to Dominic's home. Champagne flutes were filled, and soothing background music accompanied the busy chatter. It seemed all four diners felt the need to relax and were able to unwind in front of the flickering fire, with the breathtaking backdrop of the capital city — all magic and lights — sparkling beneath them.

'Is pretty nice place,' Maria said when she caught Lara on her own in the kitchen as she came to help her serve the hors d'oeuvres. 'But needs a woman's touch, huh?'

She nudged Lara knowingly.

'I think it's just that Dominic is too busy to spend much time here.' Lara was non-committal. She liked Maria but didn't intend to unburden herself to the woman. She had her pride!

'But it is such a love nest!' Maria was scandalised at the waste.

Lara laughed. 'It could be,' she agreed.

'You would like to try?'

Lara gave into Maria's wheedling. 'I'd love to try,' she admitted, before turning to carry a tray out of the kitchen door, where she almost collided with Dominic, who was coming the other way to replenish empty glasses.

He stared at her for a moment longer than was necessary or expected, a slight twist to his mouth giving his face a questioning look, as if he was trying to decide something.

Please heaven he hadn't heard that

exchange! Lara thought wildly. If he had, he would definitely think she was after what she could get.

Yet if he had, it didn't seem to have fazed him, because as the evening wore on Dominic proved to be the perfect host — not only to the Ostens, but to her as well.

After the way he had treated her at the wedding, Lara was amazed to discover he was excellent company, with a fund of amusing stories that he told at just the right rate, not hogging the limelight or cutting anyone short, but dropping them in whenever the conversation looked like flagging. He was interested in everything that was said but became really passionate when he and Paul began to talk about rebuilding Chekurov. However, their exchanges were not about business opportunities or budgets or profits, she realised, but about people, and how their lives could be transformed if the shattered country became economically successful.

He really cares, she thought, *and that's why he supports Hal!* At last it was clear it was social conscience that was Dominic's driving force and that was why he had sounded so happy when he phoned from Chekurov, and why he was so relaxed now in the Ostens' company. The two men shared the same values, she realised, and felt able to change things for the better for people. But unlike Paul, who had put his family first, Dominic appeared to be driven in a different way — he shunned all close ties to better achieve his aim. Any relationships he had were shallow and transitory.

Now that she knew the jealous power of love, she wondered whether she would be able to accept a relationship on those terms, always supposing it was offered. Once she could have given a definite answer — it had been all or nothing for her — but today, staring into the red coals, the licking flames taunting her, she knew with a sickening certainty that she would take Dominic on any terms offered.

Thank heavens her contract was nearly over, for if she stayed, she knew she would be lost.

'I love this soup, Lara!' The irrepressible Maria had noted the girl's withdrawal and sought to bring her back into the conversation.

'Good.' Lara smiled, 'I thought it would be warming for a day like today.'

'It is indeed!' Paul exclaimed, raising his glass to Lara. 'Here's to the chef.'

'Whoever he was.' She laughed at his surprise and explained the finer points of outside caterers.

The menu she had chosen was in fact a great hit, although later Lara could not remember eating a mouthful. It was as if once she had accepted that her feelings for Dominic were so strong that she would take any crumbs from under his table, she could relax and stop fighting with herself.

Dominic, too, seemed a different man, laughing and joking and smiling at her no less, rather than giving her his famous forbidding looks, in his element as he and Paul planned a glowing future for Chekurov.

Then the atmosphere changed . . .

'Why you choose that painting?' Maria was nothing if not direct, and her pursed lips demonstrated what she thought of Dominic's choice. 'Lovers want to get as close as possible to one another, not separate themselves with such veils.'

'Don't you like surrealism?'

'I like very well. I have seen travelling Dali exhibition — is very good. But this one . . . ' she waved her hand dismissively at *Les Amants*. 'It is not how lovers are — they should be open with no secrets from each other.'

Dominic gave a tense smile.

'I agree that would be the ideal, but experience tells me that doesn't often happen. Women are given to subterfuge.' He regarded the painting. 'It isn't my favourite Magritte, but I have it there for a purpose, to remind me of the duplicity of the female sex.'

'Ah, Dominic, you are a cynic!' Paul joined in the conversation, but Lara barely heard what he said. She knew to whom Dominic was referring — the fiancé who had betrayed him — and her heart sank. It seemed he was determined to see all women as dishonest cheaters, and she realised her hope that he might come to trust her was just a ridiculous dream.

They drank their coffee gathered around the fire. Paul, who became more gregarious as the evening wore on, recognised the piece of music playing in the background, and roared at Dominic to turn it up.

'Is our song!' Maria explained, and melted girlishly as her husband wrapped his arms around her ample frame, and they whirled around the flickering shadows, snuggling closer and closer.

The tempo changed, and Maria whispered something to her husband, who broke away and pulled Lara to her feet, while his wife descended on Dominic. Together they led their partners around the L-shaped room, singing and clapping along with the tune.

'Hah!' Paul cried as the music came to a stop to be replaced by a slow waltz, and once again the Ostens changed partners, leaving Lara and Dominic with no choice but to follow.

As he drew her body closer to him and began to guide her around the room, Lara's reaction was so explosive that she wondered if there wasn't another reason why Dominic was known as 'the Bomb'. She stiffened, unwilling to let him see how his nearness made her feel, but he pulled her tighter, his hand in the small of her back. She rested her head on his chest, too shy to let him see how happy she felt with their arms entwined.

She wondered if she would ever be able to let go of him, but luckily, the music helped her and as the notes faded away, she made a superhuman effort to detach herself from Dominic's arms and ask — in a voice so calm it amazed her — whether anyone wanted more coffee.

Paul and Maria shook their heads and remained arm in arm conspiratorially.

'No, we go now, we have to be up early tomorrow,' Maria said, and as Dominic went to get their coats, whispered triumphantly in Lara's ear, 'He likes you!'

Lara smiled, but said nothing. He had certainly seemed to, but she suspected it was not her he liked particularly, but any woman prepared to have an uncomplicated, uncommitted relationship. And, heaven help her, she knew she would have been willing to submit!

She gave a slight shiver. Thank goodness he was taking them all home now.

'I'll come back for you, Lara. I'd like you to clear up first, please.'

His tone left no doubt that it was an order. She felt like Cinderella after the ball, deflated and dejected. So he hadn't wanted her at all, except to play with, and she had been silly enough to react to his caress! She seemed completely unable to temper her behaviour in his presence and realised that the sooner she left his employment the better.

She said goodbye to the Ostens, Maria giving her a warm hug, and then set about clearing up. It didn't take long, and soon everything was stacked in the dishwasher or stored away, and she flopped on the sheepskin rug in front of the fire, finishing her liqueur. She felt drowsy and her eyelids drooped as sleep overtook her.

$$\star \quad \star \quad \star$$

Dominic found her there on his return. His stomach muscles had contracted when he heard Maria's comment about love nests, and as the evening had progressed, he'd come to accept that Lara was simply one of the most beautiful and entertaining women he had ever met.

He wanted her, and when they had danced together tonight, he was sure she felt the same way. He had had to think quickly to find a way to make her stay behind when he took the Ostens home, though he admitted the excuse he had used hadn't been very gallant!

Someone knelt beside Lara and encircled her with his arms. The voice that murmured in her ear was achingly familiar, and she wanted to turn to face this man of her dreams. As he rolled her towards him, dreaming turned to reality, and her green eyes fluttered open to see the harsh, darkened gaze of Dominic Leigh. His expression was grave, and she expected him to make some corrosive comment, but instead he expertly kissed her.

'Thank you for tonight,' he said. 'You were a wonderful hostess. I am so glad I chose you to be my stand-in PA.'

'I thought the reason you chose me was to keep me out of Hal's way.' She didn't intend to let him off that easily. 'And you always said I was trying to use you to get close to Hal.'

He had the grace to look ashamed.

'I know, and now I realise how wrong I was. I was judging you by the standards of others, and that was unfair.' He stroked her hair. 'Peace?'

She nodded. 'Peace,' she agreed.

'You're very forgiving.'

She had been doing all right until he started to be kind to her. She was so used to his pointed barbs that she could cope with them, but Dominic being considerate she found harder.

'I don't know why — I don't even think it was my choice.'

She looked down at her clenched fists and refused to meet his eyes. She sighed. She might just as well be truthful with him; she was hardly likely to see him again. Today had been her last day in his employment, after all.

'I just know that from the moment I met you there was something special between us.'

She shrugged and risked a quick glimpse up at him from under her long lashes before dropping her eyes again.

'Never mind, I'm sure I'll soon find someone else.' She refused to let him feel sorry for her, which would be the absolute limit.

He cupped her chin and forced her face upwards.

'Have you ever felt that way with other boyfriends?'

She sighed again. What the heck — her job was over anyway, nothing she said now could make it any worse!

'No, never. I've always been a bit of a control freak. I don't like my heart to rule my head.'

It was true, and she had just realised why.

However accepting she had believed she was regarding her adoption, deep in her subconscious an idea had been planted, an idea which equated love with babies, and babies with illegitimacy and having to give a love child away.

That was not going to happen to her — she knew she could never relinquish any baby, so she had always avoided putting herself into that situation.

Until tonight. Not that she was going to tell Dominic all that.

'Why me?'

Why deny it?

'Because I love you. I know that isn't what you want, that you like sophisticated women and transient affairs, and I'm not going to make a fuss. But you asked, so I told you . . . '

'Shut up,' he said firmly.

Then his lips crushed down upon hers and she surrendered to his arms.

9

They talked long into the night until the fire died down. Dominic found himself longing to get to know her better. He hadn't felt such a sense of joy since . . . well, since the last time he had loved and trusted a woman, he realised. And that had been many years ago.

He had forgotten how powerful the experience was, having kept his emotions firmly in check since then, and even now he was still wary. She could still let him down. But was that likely, knowing her now as he did?

As they chatted, he wondered how she'd feel if she knew that at eight o'clock the next morning he needed to be at the airport, ready to board the Airbus to France.

He hadn't told her he was going to Hal's swearing-in ceremony. Initially he'd thought it best to keep quiet about the date in case she tried to cause a scene on the day, but now he saw he must tell her and he wondered how she'd take the news. Would she think he was being disloyal, to stand support to the father who had found it politic to ignore her?

Once he would have found such an attitude naïve, but since hearing Paul and Maria's story he understood, as he had not done before, that caring for causes while being completely detached from the fate of individuals was not an intrinsically noble stance. Sometimes it was the easy option, to put public service ahead of having time to spare for fractious families.

She'd walked to the window and pulled aside the curtains to look out over the view.

'It's been snowing heavily,' she said, watching the thick flakes as they hit the glass and slid down the window. 'You don't want to get stuck in it if you're going away. I'll take a cab home.'

He argued he'd be fine, but she insisted.

'You need to get to the airport early,' she insisted and hit dial on her mobile phone to contact the company she used at work when ordering transport. 'They'll be here in a few minutes.'

He gave her a loving smile. Love . . . ? Was this love? He didn't know — it was certainly attraction, and he acknowledged he had experienced it from when he first danced with her. Physically he felt good. The tight bands he had kept around his heart as well as the general tension in his body had gone, leaving a much more relaxed mood. He could even think about Anita with equanimity now, and that, he realised, was because she no longer mattered.

Love and hate were very close emotions, he knew, and whereas he had loved her once, he wondered if by using her image as a warning against involvement, he had allowed her to stay alive in his heart for too long.

He kissed Lara's neck.

'I have to tell you something. I'm going to France tomorrow to see Hal installed.' He felt her tense, and hurried on, 'I'll be coming back on Monday, and I'll arrange something with Hal — '

She was already heading for the door.

'Is that why you're treating me like this — because you think you can keep me quiet?'

'Of course not.'

'Then why keep it a secret?'

'I just thought it would upset you and so it would be better if you didn't know.'

'Better for whom? For you and Hal I suppose!'

'Lara, please, listen to me — '

But she was already out the door and gone.

★ ★ ★

Lara stumbled as she left the flat. Only moments ago she had been so happy — almost unable to believe Dominic wanted to be with her. He hadn't

216

actually said that, of course, but she'd thought the way he'd held her, the kisses they'd shared and even the way he'd involved her in events with Paul and Maria had meant something, surely?

But just as she began to let her defences down it had become clear the real reason he'd been keeping her busy overseeing arrangements for the Ostens and romancing her, was to keep her occupied so she didn't find out about Hal's swearing-in until it was too late for her to do anything about it. Not that she would have done anything, but it seemed Dominic still suspected her of planning some dastardly revenge on Hal.

The cab drew up outside her house and she hurriedly paid the driver before rushing indoors. She walked from room to familiar room, touching loved items to give herself a sense of permanency. This was where she belonged — not in a swanky apartment overlooking the Thames. The Dunstans had never let her down, whereas everyone she had met as part of Hal's world had proved unreliable — even Henrietta, who she knew kept her apart from her everyday friends.

Dawn was breaking and she looked out over her back garden where the snow was already melting, trees plopping large drips as the temperature rose. She frowned as she noticed a set of footprints leading from her rear fence to her kitchen door and back again. What on earth was that about?

When she was a child her parents had been on first name terms with everyone who lived around them, but there was less of a neighbourhood spirit now, and Lara had no idea who owned the house behind her. But why would they want to come into her garden? If they'd needed to see her, why hadn't they come to the front door?

She walked into the kitchen and opened the back door. The problem was, as she stood on the doorstep now, she couldn't be sure that they *were* footprints. The snow had melted unevenly, and a whole caterwaul of cats seemed to have had a fight in the centre of the lawn, judging by the fur tufts and paw patterns in what remained of the snow. Perhaps it was just coincidental that a patterned line stretched from the front to the rear of her garden. Indeed, she couldn't imagine it could be anything else.

★ ★ ★

Lara spent a miserable weekend cooped up indoors. She watched Hal's acceptance speech on the news and couldn't stop herself from searching the screen for any sign of Dominic, but she didn't see him.

Don't be so stupid! she told herself, but the next day she bought every Sunday paper she could find and scanned them for his face. She was behaving like a lovesick teenager, she knew, and making herself a victim, to boot, but there was a perverse kind of release as she brooded over their short relationship.

Early on Monday morning she phoned the agency to find out what work was available.

'Not a lot, actually,' Madge admitted. 'I did have a couple of weeks down the road from you, but as I hadn't heard anything, I assumed Mr Leigh wanted you to stay on and gave it to someone else.' She went all gossipy. 'What's he like, by the way? He had one of those lovely dark brown voices.'

'He was fine,' Lara replied, which she immediately recognised would tell Madge he wasn't, because she usually indulged the older woman with a far more detailed account of her various employers.

'Well, there's no point you coming into the office, I've got everything under control. I'll call you when we get something.'

Half an hour later, Lara's phone shrilled. Expecting Madge again, she was shocked when Dominic's voice came down the line.

'Where are you, Lara, why aren't you at work?'

'My contract finished on Friday,' she replied, unwilling to go into further explantions.

'Don't be ridiculous! What am I going to do without you?'

She felt herself wilting at the sound of his voice saying such things!

'I'm sure you'll manage.'

'But I don't have to. We'll extend your contract.'

The irony wasn't lost on her that the very thing she had wanted so badly before she had realised how Dominic had been playing her, she would now refuse.

'That's not possible,' she fibbed. 'I'm starting somewhere else tomorrow.'

A silence on the line, and then, 'Say again?'

'I've another job.' She repeated the message.

'I see, and what about us? I thought

we were just starting to get along so well.'

Lara leaned back against the wall, clenching the fist that wasn't holding the receiver and took a deep breath. She knew what she had to say.

'Us? Oh, come on, Dominic, there was never really an 'us', was there? There was you and me, two people who came together for a short while, but it was hardly a great romance, was it?'

Another silence, and when he spoke his voice was like ice.

'I see. I didn't realise you saw things that way. Nor that you'd been so unhappy at Allied Markets that you would rather not work than stay another day. I've already spoken to Madge, you see, so I'm well aware you don't have another job.'

Bother Madge! Lara had forgotten how the woman lived vicariously through her younger partner. No doubt she had been on the phone to Allied Markets the moment they had stopped speaking.

'I enjoyed working at Allied Markets,' she said truthfully. 'I just think it's time for a change.'

He gave a short, harsh laugh. 'Well, if that's how you feel. Goodbye, Lara, and thank you.'

She replaced the receiver on the cradle, and hung her head in her hands. There was an ache in her stomach and a hunger in her heart.

I will get over it, she told herself, *no one dies of unrequited love. I shall just have to stop thinking about him!*

Even had she been able to do so, her best intentions were undermined by the evening television news, which had a shot of a beaming Hal, looking very pleased with himself, arriving back at Heathrow that morning with Dominic by his side.

Luckily, the phone interrupted. It was Henrietta.

'Are you watching the telly, big sis?' she demanded. 'Dad and Dom the Bomb are on.'

Dom the Bomb, Lara had forgotten

that name. Henrietta had told her how Dominic's fury at being jilted by his first love had earned him the nickname. Yet when she had backed away, rather than exploding as he had with his fiancé, he had been dangerously quiet, proving how very little he had really cared for her.

'I saw,' was all she said.

'That wasn't the only reason I phoned.' Henrietta sounded excited. 'I'm going down to Wyscom this week, and Dad wants you to come!'

So Hal deigned to meet her now there was no chance of her unfortunate start in life interfering with his appointment, did he? But did she want to see him? Hadn't she just agreed with herself that her involvement with anyone concerned with the Lawrences wasn't worth the effort?

'I'm not sure . . . '

'Don't worry about Dom!' Henrietta assumed Lara's response. 'He'll give you the time off.'

'My contract at Allied Markets

finished last week, Hen.'

'Yes, I know, but Dom told us on the plane that he intended to keep you.'

A kept woman! She could hear him saying that.

'So, are you coming?'

Lara made her decision. No matter how Hal had treated her, he was still her father, and she needed to meet the man who had given her life.

'Yes,' she said. 'I'll come.'

'Great. Can you get round here at two-thirty tomorrow? I'll drive us both down.'

So it was that at two-twenty, Lara was waved upstairs by the same doorman she'd met on her last visit. He was talking to a voluble Irish man, and recognised Lara so he didn't stop to phone Henrietta. Which threw her sister somewhat . . .

'Oh — yes — hi,' she said awkwardly when she answered the door. 'Um, come in. I've got someone here . . .' she tailed off and led the way into her drawing room. Perched elegantly on the edge of her seat was a tall, slim woman with straight black hair that hung round her face in a gleaming bob, and the angular bones and supercilious look of a top model.

'This is a friend,' Henrietta introduced Lara too quickly, obviously intent on preventing her sister from making a faux pas and admitting their real relationship.

The gorgeous one smiled, and extended a long, slim hand, but her smile didn't reach her eyes, Lara noticed, which were hard and inquisitorial. It was clear she had picked up on Henrietta's tension, and Lara could just imagine her ferreting about to find out what was behind it.

'This is Annie Kelly,' Henrietta explained. 'She wants to run a feature about Gareth and me.'

'Oh, you're a journalist?' Lara was surprised. She had thought her sister avoided all publicity, so it was strange she'd invited one into her house.

'Yes, I work for The Meeting Point,'

Annie said, which was even more surprising to Lara, because out of all the weekly celebrity publications, it was the least upmarket, and she would have expected Henrietta to be more selective.

'We met at a party,' Henrietta explained, 'and Annie had just done a feature on Bunty Prentice, who's a huge friend.'

Lara recognised the name and seemed to remember that the last time Henrietta had mentioned Bunty, friendship didn't seem to come into it at all.

'Of course, her house doesn't have the elegance of this apartment.' Annie gave a sycophantic smile. 'We could get some wonderful photographs of you and your husband here. It really is most impressive.'

'We think so.' Henrietta was lapping it up.

Lara was amazed her sister couldn't see straight through the woman, who was using the art of one-upmanship to great effect. All she could think was that

Henrietta must have been very jealous when Bunty had received her five minutes of fame, and was now determined to top her.

Annie was keen to see everything she could, so Henrietta took her on a grand tour. Lara watched as the skeletal woman, expensively dressed with Chanel and real diamonds, followed on, poking and prying wherever she could.

Lara didn't like her, and she knew the woman recognised this and that the feeling was mutual.

'So, what do you do — sorry . . . what did you say your name was?' she purred as Henrietta went to get some old photographs to show her.

'I didn't, but it's Lara.'

'She's working for Dominic Leigh at Allied Markets,' Henrietta re-entered the room, 'and I understand his pad is out of this world. Perhaps you ought to try and interview him. I'm sure Lara could ask him for you, couldn't you, La?'

'Dominic Leigh — are you close to him?' Annie seemed particularly interested.

'Hardly, I've only worked for him for four weeks,' Lara explained, at which words the journalist visibly relaxed.

'Oh, not long enough to have formed any meaningful relationship, then,' she said in a dismissive kind of way. 'What's he like these days? He used to be rather gorgeous.'

Rather gorgeous — is that how she would describe him? Yes — that and so much more!

'He's a very attractive man,' she allowed.

'Is there anyone special in his life?' Annie wanted to know all the details. 'Even as a jobbing typist you must have taken phone calls for him.'

Was there? Who knew? What she did know was that if there was someone special, it certainly wasn't her.

'I never heard of anyone,' she said, and Annie looked pleased.

'This is my card,' she said. 'Give it to

Dominic and see if he'd like to be interviewed, will you?'

Lara didn't want to admit she no longer worked for him, so she took the proffered card, and slipped it in her pocket.

When Annie Kelly had gone, Lara asked Henrietta what had induced her to agree to the publicity. 'I thought the Lawrences hated to air their business in public and she was such a ghastly woman! All that flannel about how much better this shoot would be than the one at Bunty's!'

'Lara, you're so bourgeois!' Henrietta sighed. 'We don't like negative publicity, but this shoot *will* be better than Bunty's. Her family made their money from used cars, not a very noble profession, and although they've tried to forget their past, I do love rubbing her nose in it now and then!'

'Henrietta!'

'Oh, don't look so shocked! I suppose you love everyone all the time! Well, I don't, and I especially don't like Bunty.

She was always lording it over us at boarding school, what with her father having so much money, and she's carried it right on into adult life. Well, this time, I'm going to top her!'

It seemed to Lara that there was nothing very adult about either of them, but she forbore to actually say so.

Sometimes her sister's life seemed so alien as to be incomprehensible. What did it matter if someone was richer than you if your father was a millionaire anyway? And at what age did brink-manship stop, for heaven's sake?

Annie's visit had raised another question for her, too. Just how long was she going to remain the Lawrence's guilty secret?

She had thought that once Hal had been sworn in she was to be 'rehabili-tated', but it appeared from Henrietta's behaviour that she was not.

She supposed she was still to be persona non grata until she and Hal had been properly introduced. It couldn't come soon enough.

10

They arrived at Wyscom Old Hall in time for dinner, which was difficult, because it meant the guests would be together in the dining room before Lara had formally met her father.

'It'll be OK.' Henrietta shrugged. She couldn't see what all the fuss was about.

Luckily India could, and she had arranged for herself, Hal and Lara to eat privately.

So once Lara had been shown to her room and deposited her bag, India came to fetch her and took her to the small back kitchen where she explained that she and her husband ate on the cook's night off.

It was a surprisingly unprepossessing room, with a large scrubbed pine table and a mixture of chairs, none of which matched. Lara felt awkward as she entered — how did you greet the father you had never formally met?

She was surprised to see that Hal was, if anything, even more uptight than she was. Only India, with her ready smile and natural charm, seemed to be at ease. She introduced the two, and Lara had the surreal experience of shaking her father's hand and saying, 'How do you do?'

She sat down at the table and didn't know what to say, but her father seemed to come to a decision, and suddenly he turned on the charm, and treated her like a floating voter in a marginal ward. Lara answered his questions, and in spite of herself, had to admit that when he wanted to be, her father was very charismatic.

After the meal, India rose to go.

'I'll leave you two now,' she excused herself, satisfied that they were getting along. 'You've a lot to catch up on.'

'You look like a Lawrence woman,' he said when she had gone, 'good bones.'

'And what about my mother? Is there anything of her in me?'

It was brutal, she knew, but she had to ask.

Hal Lawrence sighed, and suddenly looked every one of his fifty-nine years.

'Chloe was the most wonderful woman in the world,' he said simply. 'I adored her, but I couldn't meet her high expectations.'

'You mean you couldn't be faithful to her?'

He shifted awkwardly in his seat and put his elbows on the table.

'You wanted to know if there's anything of her in you. Well, there is. Chloe was a very straight talker, just like you.'

'I don't like subterfuge,' she agreed. 'Which is why I haven't enjoyed creeping about as if I were something to be ashamed of.' She paused, then added, 'Are you ashamed of me, Hal?'

He put his head in his hands.

'Ashamed of myself more,' he said. 'You're so like Chloe. There are no greys for you, everything is black and white. Well, I'm not like that. Grey is the colour of opportunity, the area where you can try new things and indulge yourself. I never meant to hurt Chloe — or Jane for that matter. You know about Lady Jane?'

She nodded.

'Jane was a good politician's wife.'

Poor woman, thought Lara, *what an epitaph: a good politician's wife!*

'She understood chaps like me, and as long as I didn't humiliate her, she was happy that I had other ... friends — '

'Female friends?' Lara was not going to let him get away with anything.

'Female friends,' he agreed, nodding. 'But we weren't in love, though we were very fond of each other, and probably would have rubbed along happily if I hadn't met your mother.'

'What was she like?'

'Mercurial, stainless, special ... ' He shook his head. 'I have never met anyone like her, before or since, and I knew I had to have her, had to possess her so no other man could. The trouble was, she wouldn't play ball, it was marriage or nothing.'

'Even though she knew you were married?'

He sighed. 'She didn't, not at first, and when she found out . . . well, it was a bit late by then.'

So her mother hadn't set out to break up a home, Lara was pleased to learn. But by the time she realised the truth she must have been expecting her elder daughter.

'Somehow Jane found out about us, even though we'd tried to hide our tracks and had given you up for adoption. She divorced me, and Chloe and I married.'

'Why did you leave Chloe?'

'Politics. She couldn't keep her mouth shut.'

He saw his daughter's shocked expression and hurried on to explain. 'Sometimes, to get what you want in politics, you have to support people you wouldn't normally support, do things you wouldn't choose to do, vote for an outcome that is not your own. Chloe couldn't see that, and 'being political' began to wear her down.'

Hal was fidgeting in his chair, and she wondered what was making him uncomfortable.

'What was it that started it all — your parting, I mean?'

She saw his shoulders slump.

'You did,' he said at last. 'She became pregnant before I was divorced. If it had got out all hell would have broken loose, so I sent her away and then arranged for you to be adopted.'

'My father — Dan Dunstan — he worked for you, didn't he?'

'He worked a farm on the estate.' Hal nodded.

'And had you arranged for my adoption even before I was born?'

'No, of course not!' Hal clearly found it hard to believe anyone would ask such an obvious question. 'You might have been a boy!'

The shock of his answer left Lara momentarily speechless. He realised he'd made a mistake.

'Estates pass down to sons,' he tried to explain, 'and even if I only married Chloe after the birth, it would legitimise any child we'd had out of wedlock.'

'Like me?'

'Well, yes, if it had been politically expedient to do so. As it was, I didn't dare have any more black marks against my name, so as you weren't a boy, we decided to have you adopted.'

So it all boiled down to a question of gender. If she had been born a Larry instead of a Lara, this would have been her home.

Thank heavens it wasn't! she thought. Imagine if she had been left to Hal's tender mercies — and she would have been when he moved on from her mother — what kind of person would she have grown up to be? A male version of Henrietta, she supposed — basically OK, but with no social conscience and a sense of entitlement.

Now she saw she had been wrong in thinking Dominic wanted to ape Hal's behaviour. In fact they couldn't be more unalike. That was the difference Henrietta had sensed between Dominic and the Lawrences — Dominic fought for rights, the Lawrences still harked back to a kind of droit du seigneur.

'But you said I was the reason why you and Chloe eventually parted.'

He nodded. 'Yes, she couldn't forgive me, you see, for making her give you up. Oh, she loved Hen madly, but whenever she looked at her she was reminded that somewhere she had another daughter, and it began to eat away at her. That's when she started making comments about politicians not being worth the sacrifice she'd had to make.'

So her mother had missed her. Lara felt a pang for the young woman who'd had to give her baby up — while at the same time recognising she was glad it had not been easy. It showed her mother must have loved and valued her after all.

'I'm sorry you feel you were let down . . . ' Hal sounded sheepish, but she noted he did not take responsibility for her adoption. He had not said I'm sorry *I* let you down. The typical politician's language of unaccountability.

'It's OK.' She rose to go. 'I couldn't have had better parents than the Dunstans.'

He looked at her closely, as if to see if she was being sarcastic, and when he realised she was not, looked pensive. 'No, I don't suppose you could have,' was all he said.

India Lawrence was hovering in the hall anxiously.

Waiting to see I'm all right, Lara thought, *waiting to comfort me, but I don't need it*.

She smiled, and India linked her arm through hers and smiled back.

'Do you understand him better now?'

Lara nodded. 'Yes, it's as you said, he's weak.'

'That's not quite what I said,'

protested India, 'though I can see why you might think it. In many ways he is a fine man — '

'You can still say that?' Lara was amazed by her loyalty.

India patted her arm. 'You're young,' she said, 'and idealistic. I was once, but I've learned life is not always as straightforward as we might like. We don't necessarily fall in love with the people who are best for us, we just fall in love.

'The important thing is knowing what's important to you, whether a man means so much to you that you can put up with sides of his behaviour you'd rather he didn't exhibit. I made that choice and it hasn't always been easy, but I would rather be with him than without him, and we have been married for nearly twenty years now.'

Wise words, thought Lara, as she followed India's directions back to her bedroom.

She wanted to be alone to think. She had dreamed an impossible dream, imagining herself as part of Hal's family, only to find herself relieved that she had not actually been brought up by him. Life as Hal's daughter would have been a nightmare for her — she was different from Henrietta, and much too like Chloe to have been able to accept his irregular arrangements. She could see they would have had right royal battles about his behaviour — a hero with feet of clay.

And what of Dominic?

Hadn't she built him up to be something he was not? He had promised her nothing, but she had chosen to read into his kisses something more, only to have her hopes dashed.

India was right, you needed to keep your feet on the ground even while your heart was in the clouds, and clinically assess what a relationship would give you and whether you could live with that. Lara recognised that in walking away from Dominic she had made the right decision, because she could never live like India, whose sunny smile belied her sad eyes. She was a woman who not only had to suffer her husband's indiscretions, but also had to hide her feelings lest she made him feel guilty — and then resentful.

Someone had unpacked her clothes, Lara saw, and laid out her nightdress. The curtains were pulled and the dimmed glow from the old-fashioned wall lights showed the room at its best: dark oak floors with a scattering of Persian rugs, a large tester bed, and solid old furniture that smelled of polish and clearly had been there for hundreds of years.

There was a pile of old society magazines on the bedside table, and she lay back on the bed and started to flick through the first of them in a desultory sort of way. It seemed to consist of beautiful young ladies with bare shoulders and expensive rocks on their fingers posing demurely for engagement pictures at the front. At the back, pages of photographs of the rich and famous enjoying themselves at notable events

— Ascot, Glyndebourne, a party to celebrate an eighteenth birthday and another to celebrate a make of champagne.

Many of the faces appeared again and again, and she wondered how they found the time, before realising that this was actually exactly how they did spend all their time. Once or twice she glimpsed Hal and India, or Henrietta and a number of different escorts, but initially most of the faces meant nothing to her.

Then, on the last page, there he was . . . *Mr Dominic Leigh and friend*, said the caption, and there he was, devastatingly handsome in a dinner jacket, and on his arm, a small, smiling woman, looking straight at the camera.

His partner wasn't beautiful in the accepted sense of the word. Her hair was too mousey and her face too round for that, but she had a shining smile and carried off her spiky hair and huge and obviously fake diamond earrings with aplomb. She looked fun, Lara decided with a pang, and noted Dominic was looking at her and laughing.

She had been pretty bored with the reading matter up until then, but now gathered up all the magazines and let the pages run through her thumb just to find any more photos of him. So he had a permanent girlfriend . . . well, he had kept her well hidden.

She wondered why, and her suspicious mind came up with the answer: it must have been that in his determination to protect Hal, he was so committed to controlling his erstwhile daughter that he had always intended to pretend to have feelings for her to get round her if he needed to.

She shivered. The room was cold and draughty, but the ice in her heart was about more than that. She slipped under the covers fully dressed, which was a mistake.

* * *

When she woke up the old house was quiet, or as quiet as an old house ever could be. There were creaks and rattles in the night, but no sound of life. She shivered as she pulled on her night-dress, and then swore as she realised she had forgotten to pack a dressing gown. The bathroom had been pointed out to her down the hall, and she realised that she'd just have to freeze all the way there and back. She wasn't worried about meeting anyone — her watch showed it was two in the morning, and she doubted anyone else was awake.

The heavy oak door creaked alarm-ingly as she opened it, and she tiptoed barefoot down the passageway.

She found the right door without any problem, and did what she had to as quickly as she could, the bathroom being even colder than her bedroom. She'd read county types were a hardy lot, and now she knew why. They kept their houses like ice boxes so only the toughest would survive!

She hurried silently back to her bedroom, catapulting straight into a fellow guest as he walked out of his bedroom door!

When Henrietta had told her Hal had invited a number of people to stay over the weekend she had been pleased, thinking he intended to introduce her to his friends. She realised that in her earlier meeting with Hal, they hadn't addressed how her presence should be broached, but it appeared she was about to be put to the test with one of the visitors already.

'I'm sorry!' she whispered to the shadowy figure in the doorway.

His head jerked up at the sound of her voice, and suddenly she was being pulled into the bedroom. She was about to scream when her eyes grew accustomed to the gloom of the room, and she realised she was staring into the granite face of Dominic Leigh.

'What are you doing here?' they said in unison.

'I was invited,' he said shortly.

'Me too. If I'd known you were here I'd've stayed away, no matter how much I wanted to meet Hal.'

'Yes, you made your feelings very plain on the phone,' he snapped, 'you don't need to go over them again.'

'I wasn't the one who started this, you grabbed me, remember!'

He was grasping her firmly on her upper arms, but made no attempt to release her.

'I apologise.' He gave a formal apology. 'It was a shock to hear your voice, and I had to be sure.'

'Well now you are, perhaps you'll let me go.'

The cold had given Lara goose bumps before he touched her, but as his hard fingers pressed into the bare flesh of her arms, she felt another sensation — a mixture of fire and ice which made her shiver with anticipation and despair.

What was it India had said? That you needed to know how much a man meant to you before you could decide whether you could accept the sacrifice of loving

248

him. To that Lara would add the need to be alone when you determined your answer, because standing next to him now, she knew it would be hard to deny Dominic anything.

'Let me go!' she said, frightened her fierce feelings would overcome her scruples if she stayed any longer.

'Do you want that, Lara? Do you really?'

His voice was deep and taunting, and he took a step closer so he was staring down at her.

'You seemed to enjoy my company before I went to France, and I don't understand why you were so angry about my supporting Hal. You knew that was my priority.'

'It wasn't your going I minded, it was the way you kept it from me. It was so deceitful.'

'I had to be sure you wouldn't be able to cause any problems and — '

'So because you didn't trust me, you pretended to be attracted to me. Apart from being thoroughly dishonest, it was 'also unfair to your girlfriend.'

'Girlfriend?' He looked puzzled.

'Oh, don't play the innocent with me! I know you have one. I've seen her photograph with you in The Meeting Point.'

He crossed his arms over his chest. 'And you're jealous, is that it?'

'Don't flatter yourself! At least Hal is honest about his liaisons and India knows about them.'

'And that makes it all right, does it?'

'Of course it doesn't, but at least she was given a choice to accept it or not, which I wasn't.'

She turned and made to go, but he caught hold of her again.

'I didn't tell you because I don't *have* a girlfriend. And I ensured you didn't go to the swearing in because I thought it might hurt you to be 'so near and yet so far'. The whole family were present — India, Henrietta, even Hannah — seeing Hal with both your half-sisters, I didn't want you to feel like an outsider.'

Could it be true? She wanted it to be true!

'What about the girl in the photos with you?'

'I've never pretended to be other than what I am — I told you when we met there had been women who saw me as a meal ticket for life — but I found that a pretty unattractive proposition, so I made sure no one got the opportunity to move in on me.'

She began to protest, but he held up his hand.

'No, hear me out,' he said. 'I haven't had a long-standing partner for years. You must have realised that, seeing my apartment. There's no sign of a woman there, is there? It's pretty impersonal as I don't like clutter in my business life, and that's how I class the apartment — as part of my work.' He paused. 'You may not think very highly of me, but I do actually have standards.'

'So who is the woman?'

'Come on, Lara, you worked for me long enough to know the amount of events I get invited to, not just business but also charitable functions, race meetings, balls . . . They're not my idea of fun, but attending them goes with the territory, and the expectation is that one will escort a partner.'

'What's that got to do with anything?'

'If you'd just stop interrupting and let me finish . . . I've told you I didn't want to give any woman the impression I was an available asset, but that did make it rather difficult when I needed an escort. I don't want to turn up with different women all the time, and neither do I want someone who would embarrass me by behaving in a predatory way all evening. So I came up with the idea of writing it into the job description.'

'What? You've got a job description for an escort?' Lara felt she was losing the plot.

'No — for my PA. You never saw it because the job wasn't advertised, but when Ashley came to work for me, part of her duties was to accompany me on semi-official business. That's who I'm with in all the pictures.'

Suddenly it made sense, but she had to be sure. 'What does she look like, Ashley?'

He had to think for a moment.

'Let me see . . . she's about five feet two inches, neat figure, short brown hair — she could never keep a hat on because there wasn't anything to pin it to — and a roundish face.'

Relief flooded through her! He was telling the truth. And she also saw that his words gave away more than he said. It was impossible to believe that anyone who had to think so hard and then gave such a commonplace description, could be in any way attracted to the person he was talking about.

'It was great while it lasted,' he said, 'but once she became a mother she wanted to be home in the evenings, so I've tended to give my apologies for most recent invitations. However, I shall have to find a new partner. As Hal has pointed out, I need to keep networking if I'm to be any help to him in Europe.'

'Do you always do what Hal wants?'

'No. Why do you ask?' He cocked his head on one side and regarded her with interest.

'Well, he asked you to hire me, didn't he?' she asked. 'Wanted you to keep me out of the limelight until his appointment?'

He looked surprised. 'Not at all,' he said, 'I made that decision myself. I tried to convince myself I was doing it to protect Hal, but I was lying. I couldn't stop thinking about you after we met, and I wanted to get to know you better.'

She shivered again.

'You're freezing,' he said. 'Here, put this round you,' and he pulled the throw from the bed and draped it round her. She tried to take a step forward, but swaddled in the thick folds of velour she tripped and fell headlong onto the four poster. With her hand trapped by her sides she landed face down, unable to save herself.

'Darling girl, are you all right?'

He was beside her in a trice, gently rolling her onto her back and cradling her in his arms. He stroked her hair out of her eyes.

'I couldn't bear it if I'd hurt you.'

'P-thew!' Lara blew the fibres from her mouth. 'Yes, I'm fine, really.' And how could she not be when she was his 'darling girl'?

He gave a relieved chuckle. 'Thank goodness! It would be just my luck if having found the one woman I can actually trust and love, I accidentally crowned her!'

'So you do finally trust me and believe it had never been my intention to harm Hal?'

'I do. I did doubt you, but I was judging you on the actions of someone I knew a long time ago. Now I know you are the one woman I want to spend the rest of my life with.'

'Oh, Dominic, I want that, too!'

She lifted her face to his kiss.

Lara crept out of Dominic's room at dawn.

What had she done? She had always promised herself she wouldn't be like Chloe, but when it came to it, she had found love too strong.

Before he would let her go, Dominic had insisted she agreed a date for a quiet registry office wedding as soon as possible.

'We're meant to be together,' he had said, and she had agreed. They decided not to broadcast their feelings too soon: time enough after they were married.

Breakfast was served in the grand dining room, with dishes keeping the eggs and bacon and black pudding warm, and everyone helping themselves. As India wasn't up, only Dominic understood how intimidating the household could be, and she was glad he was beside her, smoothing the way.

'My PA,' he said when anyone asked

who she was, as it was clear Hal did not intend to introduce her as his daughter. Her father might be prepared to recognise her, but he seemed determined no one else should.

'Coming for a walk?' Dominic asked no one in particular, and only Lara accepted his offer.

She borrowed Wellingtons from the boot room, and wrapped up warmly with scarf and gloves. They walked through the sleeping gardens, across the leaf mulch under the beech trees and out into the open along the muddy track that led to the home farm.

Out of sight of the big house he slipped his arm through hers, and her world was complete. The dry leaves crunched under their feet, and occasionally a twig would fall with a crack from a tree as they passed, or a squirrel would have a mad moment and perform a dazzling acrobatic display before chasing off into the bushes.

'I'm off to Chekurov next week,' he said as they walked, 'but you'll come back to the office the following Monday, won't you?'

'Of course,' she agreed and he pulled her round to face him and kissed her, their frozen breath making steaming patterns around them.

They walked on hand-in-hand. It was very cold, the brown furrows of the field white with frost, and suddenly a fox raced across the horizon. They laboured on over the hills following the rutted path, past a walled kitchen garden where rows of beans had gone to seed and bloated pumpkins had passed their best, coming upon the home farm almost unawares as they rounded a corner.

It was a large, welcoming, brick building, not grand but not unimposing, with a black Labrador by the back gate, and washing stiff with frost standing to attention on the line. Smoke snaked from the chimney, and the sound of music coming from the open kitchen window was interrupted by such a beautifully enunciated announcement, that Lara was sure they were listening to the BBC.

'The path forks here.' Dominic made to follow the easier route across the fields, but Lara pulled him back, enchanted by the overgrown path that meandered past a swollen stream, and reluctantly he followed.

It was a mistake.

The way became very muddy, and what had seemed a secret place soon opened out to an uninviting track running alongside the main road to Wyscom. Still, they were luckier than the other walkers they saw who were having to tramp along the Tarmac, having parked their cars in the church-yard.

'Let's go back,' he said, but she'd seen a flash of green in the trees ahead, and wanted to go on to investigate.

She had read in the national papers that there were now flocks of natura-lised parakeets in Surrey, their forebears having escaped captivity and discovered they could survive very well in the warm south east, and she hoped she might see one. Unfortunately, the green flash proved to be a crisp packet that had got caught in a tree! So they retraced their steps, panting as they toiled back up the steep hill.

★   ★   ★

The weekend passed in a dream for Lara, her newly found happiness with Dominic making her less judgmental of Hal's behaviour, and more accepting of what he had done.

For his part, he clearly took to his older daughter, to her feistiness and independence, qualities which reminded him of her mother — and which his other daughters, brought up wanting for nothing, lacked.

Dominic left first, having decided Lara should return to London with Henrietta as originally planned. Lara didn't even tell her sister of the change in her circumstances, wanting to protect her privacy and get to know the

Lawrences better before she opened up to them completely.

'You'll miss him.' India had found her standing in the library, watching his car drive away.

She turned round, startled by the woman's perception.

'Don't worry, no one else suspects, and your secret is safe with me.' Hal's wife smiled. 'The only reason I noticed was because years of being married to Hal have made me attuned to the signs. I know when there's someone new, and I can see if it's really love. With you it is, isn't it?'

Lara nodded.

'I like Dominic,' India continued, 'And I can see you are good for each other. I hope it works out for you.'

Lara had warmed to India over the weekend. She was more understanding than the rest of her overpowering family, and more caring. Perhaps it was her own unhappiness that had made her empathetic, a quality singularly lacking in Hal.

'I've enjoyed my stay, India, thank you.'

'And we've enjoyed having you.' India held Lara's hands in her own. 'Don't be a stranger; this is your home now, too.'

But it wasn't. Lara was pleased to have met them, but she knew now that the Lawrences were not her family. There was more to relationships than blood, and she would always be the Dunstans' daughter, no matter who her birth parents had been.

11

Lara was glad she was off the next week, as it gave her a chance to collect her thoughts and decide what to do. She would of course return to work at Allied Markets, but she was experienced enough to see that having a relationship such as theirs, she and Dominic would find it hard to work together.

She had worked for companies before where grand passions had interfered with the day-to-day running of the business, and was determined that should not happen in their case. They would need to talk about how they would manage to keep their personal and professional lives separate, and she rather suspected that would mean not working together at all — because if they were in close contact, she didn't see how they would be able to keep their hands off each other!

She also used the week to make a concerted effort to carry out a rather late autumn clearing of her garden. It wasn't her favourite pastime, but she felt she owed it to Mr Dunstan, who had been a keen gardener, to at least keep it tidy.

She worked solidly through the day, and was surprised to see a man in a black wool coat and shiny shoes watching her from the garden behind.

'Can I help you?' she asked, but he looked disconcerted and shook his head.

'I'm an estate agent,' he explained. 'Just looking at the different views.'

That was interesting. She might want to sell her house in the not too distant future, and she'd get an idea of what it might fetch when her neighbour's was advertised. The houses were all much of a muchness round here.

Woah! She pulled herself up short. She was getting a bit ahead of herself, she admitted. Perhaps she had better

wait until Dominic actually made his
intentions known!

* * *

The week sped by, and she was looking
forward to seeing him again.

'Don't bother coming to the airport,'
he'd said. 'I'll be getting in at a really
God-forsaken hour, so why don't you
come over about eleven and we can
have brunch and read the Sunday
papers . . . if we can't think of anything
better to do.' He'd grinned as he said it,
and she had laughed.

So she was surprised when the phone
shrilled her awake at six o'clock. It was
still dark outside, and she fumbled
before her sleepy hand found the
phone.

'Hello?'

'Oh, so you're still there, I thought
you might have been put up in some
hotel to keep you away from the rest of
the braying press!' Dominic's voice was
harsh and angry.

265

'Wh-what?'

'You heard, and don't try and play the innocent with me! Lord knows how I could have let myself fall for it — all that tosh about values and family and trust. Did you enjoy stringing me along, Lara? Did it make you feel powerful to have hoodwinked the biggest cynic of all? I bet it did!'

She struggled into an upright position and turned on her bedside lamp.

'Dominic, what on earth are you talking about?'

'You, selling your story to the press!' His words made no sense! 'That was your plan all along, just as I said, wasn't it? To get close to me so you could get close to Hal!'

'Dominic, please calm down and tell me — '

'Don't tell me to calm down! I thought that once Hal was in post you'd be unable to damage him, and then, fool that I was, I began to trust you, so I took my eye off the ball. I should have realised what you were actually after was money, and that scandal sells papers. It doesn't matter to editors that Hal has the job, they can still undermine him with the tittle-tattle of snakes like you!'

Lara gave a wild cry. Why was he talking to her like this, what had she done to deserve such scorn? She knew nothing about papers, and wanted him to know that, but he wouldn't listen.

'It's no good denying it, Lara, I've got the paper here in front of me, and there's no one else it could be. Your story's on the front page, with a complete resumé of your life. Only close family knew about you and Hal, and then there are the pictures — of you in the garden — how could they have got those if not through you?'

She remembered the niggling events at the back of her house . . . the flash that she now realised must have been a camera, the footprints and the 'estate agent' and tried to explain.

'Oh, how very convenient, telling me this now! If you were so worried, why didn't you mention it at the time? I'll tell you why, because you arranged it!'

'I didn't, I didn't!'

'Well, the clincher is the picture of you in the woods near the home farm. That's why you wanted to walk by the road, wasn't it? So your friends, the photographers in the churchyard, could get a good picture of you on Hal's land.'

It was like some terrible nightmare!

'Dominic, I swear I know nothing about all this!' But he wouldn't listen.

'Drop it, Lara. I think we've said all we're ever going to need to say.' He paused and then, 'I trusted you!' He spat the word out before slamming down the receiver.

Lara sat trembling for seeveral minutes.

She had to get up, to go to the newsagents and get the offending paper. She ran to the bathroom, and as she passed the hall she heard a low mumbling sound outside her house. Then the door bell rang, and she stood behind a curtain to peep out. Quite a crowd was gathering in her front garden — reporters all.

★ ★ ★

She saw a lot of them over the next few days.

They phoned her constantly, offering her first money and then lightly veiled threats when she turned them down — *other people won't be as understanding as we are.*

They stuffed messages through her letterbox, and paid her neighbours to let them camp out with cameras in their houses, so she daren't put a foot out of doors. She was under siege, and when a particularly persistent man climbed over the garden fence and into the back garden — not for the first time as she now knew — she called the police.

They came in to discuss the situation, and Lara realised there was little they could do. She also learned, from the way they treated her, that she was now notorious, someone to point out and whisper about, and she didn't like the feeling at all.

Under siege in her home, Dominic's contemptuous accusations reverberated around in her mind. How could he believe she had done this — betrayed both him and her father?

She hoped he loved her, but lovers trusted one another and he had denounced her without a thought. His reaction demonstrated he had not really held any deep feelings for her, and the knowledge hurt her more than she could have believed possible.

She wasn't eating and found it difficult to sleep; tortured dreams waking her to remember the reality and loneliness of her present situation.

She had tried to phone Henrietta the day the news broke, but her sister wouldn't come to the phone, and it was left to Gareth to tell her, as gently as he could, that his wife didn't want to see her again.

She didn't try India after that; sure

she would get a similar response.

Through it all, she felt her heart was breaking. She had thought she'd found the love of her life, just as Chloe had done, and now, like her mother, she was experiencing the pain of rejection. And there was no escape from it — the aching loss which filled her every waking moment and flooded her eyes with tears at the slightest provocation — a memory, a newspaper photograph, the waltz that had been playing on the radio as they danced. How could the joy of last week have come to this?

It hadn't been difficult to find out where the story had come from. A familiar silver car had drawn up outside on the Sunday, and a very self-important Malcolm had clambered out of the passenger seat and marched up to her front door with a driver, the erstwhile 'estate agent' turned photographer.

'Lara, let me in!' he bellowed, but she had made the connection. She recognised the car as the one Dominic had noticed at the end of her road, and then it all fell into place . . .

Malcolm's insistence he would look into her past, the car she had seen driving away from her house — it was his, of course, how had she not realised that? When she picked up the paper that he had stuffed through her letterbox, having refused to open the door, she saw she had even been right in her belief that she and Maria were being followed. There was a picture of the two of them shopping, and even one of her with Dominic and the Ostens leaving the Wyscom Hotel.

The Truth Hal Lawrence Didn't Want You To Know, screamed the headline, and in the corner was a picture of Malcolm, looking remarkably smug. So he'd made it to the nationals, thought Lara — but at what a cost?

The story was sensationalised out of all proportion. There was no mention of her happy life with the Dunstans. Rather she was shown as a lonely, unloved orphan, hidden from view like

272

the legendary malformed Earl of Glamis Castle. Hal was shown as a callous, uncaring father who refused to acknowledge his second daughter.

Malcolm phoned her next, and when she berated him for his behaviour he lashed back about her privileged life and how it was only fair he had a chance to make some money, too.

'Out of your family?' She was aghast.

'You weren't so devoted to family when I wanted to move in.'

'That's different, it's married people who live together — ' she began, but he interrupted.

'Oh, and when did you get married? I saw you coming home in the early morning in your evening clothes, so don't tell me you hadn't spent the entire night out!'

She felt repelled by him and told him so before slamming down the receiver, after which she unplugged her landline and turned off her mobile.

It will be a nine-day wonder, she comforted herself, *tomorrow it will be yesterday's news.*

But by the end of the week the story showed no signs of abating, and she begin to worry. The broadsheets had taken up the story, and she had been unable to get out of the house all week because of the reporters lying in wait. It even reached the TV news, and she saw Hal muttering a terse, 'No comment' as he caught a plane back to Europe.

Hal's enemies were making great capital out of the disclosures, and it was being said he might have to resign. Pundits chewed over what a disaster this would be for Europe, particularly for the poorer countries, and deplored the fact that gossip was being used to threaten a political appointment.

Dominic had tried to make her realise how important Hal was to countries like Chekurov, and as she listened to the commentators discussing Hal's political record, she acknowledged he had been right. Hal saw opportunities and took them, and if he sometimes had to gain support from dubious souls or hurt people's feelings, so be it. The end justified the means as far as he was concerned.

Although Lara didn't completely concur, she could see her father had some special talent and seemed to know just how far he could go, which causes were worth pursuing and which were not. It would indeed be a great loss if he had to resign.

What could she do?

Lara had never felt so alone, not even after the Dunstans had died. There was no one she could turn to. She couldn't trust reporters after the way they had behaved, and the Lawrences and Dominic had turned their backs on her.

It was this latter that hurt the most — the way Dominic had not believed her. She had thought he had learned to trust her as she had him, but she had been wrong. Life was not as black and white as that.

Who was it who had said that to her?

Oh, yes . . . Hal. She was discovering it was true, nothing was set in stone

— though at night, when she dreamed of Dominic and cried in the moonlight because it was over, she wished it were. If she were made of stone her heart wouldn't ache in that numbing, disabling way, and her life might have some meaning again.

She had to keep her curtains drawn all the time now, to stop cameras stealing secret photos of her, so the kitchen was gloomy with the blinds down as she fed the washing machine.

She slipped her hand into the pocket of the pair of jeans she had worn on the drive down to Wyscom, and pulled out a small piece of card.

Annie Kelly, she read, and remembered the journalist she had met at Henrietta's only a week ago. She wondered . . .

She hadn't taken to the woman, there had been something much too calculating about her and the way she had laid it on with a trowel for Hen's benefit had been really over the top. Still, her sister had seemed to lap it up, so perhaps she was being overly sensitive. The truth was, Annie Kelly was the only person she knew in the media apart from Malcolm. She looked at the number on the card and made a decision.

She would phone the reporter and see if she could help.

'Hello?'

It was a mobile number and Lara got through straight away, recognising the husky voice that answered irritably. However, the tone changed the moment she heard who it was, and became the same slavish flatterer Lara remembered. It was interesting to be on the receiving end this time — at Henrietta's, Annie had made it only too clear that Lara was far too unimportant to warrant her attention.

'I'm sure we could do a wonderful article about you,' cooed Annie. 'I thought when we met how photogenic you were. I could kick myself for not recognising the likeness between you and Henrietta, of course, but when I'm working I focus all my attention on the person I'm going to write about, otherwise I probably would have done.'

Lara forbore to point out that Annie had steadfastly ignored her once she had ascertained she wasn't important, and instead explained what she wanted.

'This isn't about me,' she said, 'it's about Hal. He's being crucified by the press, and it's very unfair. I always knew I was adopted, and I had a wonderful childhood. I want people to know that so they stop carping on at him, and I want it published as soon as possible.'

'We're not like the newspapers, Lara. Even though we're a weekly publication we prepare our copy weeks in advance. This isn't a quick fix.'

'Then I'm not interested. Forget it.'

She was about to put the receiver down, but Annie quickly changed her tune, as if she knew what a coup she was being offered.

'Look, I'll see what can be done,' she promised. 'We'll publish as soon possible, and run an advertising campaign beforehand saying how you want to set the record straight and how wonderful Hal is, so people know what's coming. It's such a topical story, I'm sure I can square it with my boss.'

Lara felt a glimmer of hope, but wished she could be more confident she was doing the right thing. She knew the old joke about celebrity magazines, that whenever anyone agreed to be featured in them dire things happened to the subjects within weeks of publication — usually, it seemed, a relationship break-up.

At least that couldn't happen to her, as her relationship had ended the day her story had hit the papers. Should she go ahead?

With no one to advise her she could only trust her instincts, and she couldn't see any other way of getting her message across.

★ ★ ★

Things happened very quickly after that. Because she was practically trapped in her own house, and also because her surroundings were not considered stylish enough for the soft focus photo shoot they were planning, the magazine sent a car to fetch her, plus an escort to get her through the press pack.

She was whisked away to a Palladian mansion in Berkshire, once the home of the great and good and recently at the centre of a celebrated wedding, now an impressive but anonymous hotel. Annie was there waiting and hurried her away to the elegant suite of rooms the magazine had booked, eager to keep her out of reach of rival journalists.

Lara had given the magazine her dress size, and a stylist spent some time working through a huge number of designer clothes with her, until Annie made the final choice on what should be worn for the photo shoot.

'They're a bit tight,' Annie pursed her lips. It was clear that to her, to carry extra weight was a cardinal sin. 'Still, we can always pin you at the back if the zips won't meet.'

Lara was surprised, as she hadn't been able to eat or sleep since the story broke. Her sense of loss was acute and her mind felt blank and empty. She kept imagining she heard his voice, and jumped whenever the phone rang. She cried a lot when alone, and didn't care what the future held if it was a future without Dominic.

Now she made no comment and let the stylists fashion her hair and paint her face, but couldn't raise any interest in the procedure. She was here for a purpose — to help Hal — and everything else she found pretty meaningless.

'How's Dominic?' Annie asked guilelessly at the end of the day. They were lounging in deep armchairs in front of an open fire that crackled in the carved stone fire place of the main reception room. 'Has he got a girlfriend in tow?'

'No — I don't think so. I don't

know.' Lara didn't want to discuss him.

'He's such a stickler for what he considers good behaviour.' Annie had a dreamy look in her eyes. 'Though he's so gorgeous, I suppose he can be forgiven everything.'

'I suppose so,' Lara agreed, and her bottom lip trembled.

Annie was watching her so closely it made her uncomfortable. The woman probed a little deeper.

'He doesn't go in for long term relationships, does he? Love 'em and leave 'em seems to be his motto.'

'It's not like that!' Lara sprung to his defence. 'He just has to be able to believe in people. Apparently a girl let him down once, so he's very wary about trusting women.'

Annie put her head on one side and gave an enigmatic smile as she digested this. 'So how does he feel about your notoriety?' she asked.

Lara was beginning to hear warning signals. She wasn't here to talk about her erstwhile boss, and wished Annie would stop. She supposed the woman was simply trying to build up rapport, but really, Dominic was nothing to do with her now.

'Dominic is a very private man, he hates publicity of any kind,' she said. 'But I was only his secretary, so I can't see he'd care one way or the other.'

'Oh, I thought you went out with him? Didn't you accompany him when that east European couple were in England? I thought there was a picture of you all in the papers?'

'In a business capacity,' was all Lara said, but her pale face and sad eyes said more.

Lara had to sign a contract, and when she saw the amount of money they were offering, her eyes seemed to double in size, and she pointed to the figure speechlessly. No wonder Henrietta hadn't minded that The Meeting Point was a more downmarket version of celebrity stories. It was clear that to make up for their lowly position they had to give bigger incentives.

Annie construed Lara's action as one of negotiation, and upped the original offer, to which Lara could only nod in stunned silence.

So keen was the magazine to keep Lara away from rival bidders that they made her stay at the hotel for three days, and then drove her home where she was delighted to see the press posse was no longer on her doorstep.

New stories were breaking, and the knowledge that Lara was under contract to The Meeting Point — the magazine had already begun its advertising campaign — had combined to make her yesterday's news.

Lara was pleased to be able to get out to the shops again without causing undue interest, and wandered down the aisles of the supermarket making her selections.

That was the first time it happened — the floor seemed to rush up and meet her, and she thought if she didn't sit down she would fall down. She leant over her trolley to steady herself and waited until the feeling passed, before completing her task and hurrying home.

The second time was when she was tidying up the garden, and she bent down to pull at a stubborn root. Again that whooshing feeling, and this time she did sit down, heavily, on the damp grass.

The third occasion she was in the bath, and she stumbled out as quickly as she could, cross that she had obviously made the water so hot she had come over all faint.

Clearly the stress of the last few weeks was proving too much for her, and she wished things would revert to that quieter pace of life she had known before she started to search for her real identity. She hoped that her revelations to The Meeting Point would start that process.

Annie was as good as her word, and the article on Lara and Hal was published in record quick time. Commentators had been saying that if Hal could hang on until Christmas, it was likely he would keep his job because by then the impressive results he was getting would be more widely known.

The trouble was, his enemies were doing all they could to keep the story alive — the more so since they had heard Lara was going to come out supporting her father.

The Meeting Point changed all that. The prose might have been in Annie's flowery form, but the message was clear: Hal had made the right decision in putting Lara up for adoption, and however much it had grieved him (*Ha!* thought Lara) he had waited until his daughter wanted to see him, rather than contacting her himself, because he didn't want to disturb her life.

'I'm so fortunate,' Lara was quoted as saying, 'I've had two wonderful fathers, and now I have sisters as well.'

The photographs of Lara against the backdrop of timeless opulence at the stately home added point to this story about statesmen and class, and she had to admit she looked good. Her face had a soft fulfilment, and her well-rounded figure showed off the couturier designs to perfection. But then, with an army of stylists, hairdressers and make-up artists in the background, she supposed it would have been difficult for anyone to photograph badly.

There was no doubt that Lara's endorsement of her father had the power to silence his critics, but there was another side to the story that made her feel quite sick when she saw it . . . because Annie had not confined her comments to the Lawrence family, but also included mention of Dominic . . .

Dominic Leigh, owner of Allied Markets, is a close family friend of the Lawrences, and acted as go-between in their negotiations with Lara, she had written. *Dominic is committed to the work Hal is undertaking in Europe, and with his devastating good looks, it would not have been surprising if this latter day Cinderella hadn't fallen a little bit in love with him. All Lara will say is that they are close. He stayed with her at the recent reunion at Wyscom Old Hall, and she has acted as hostess at his romantic penthouse apartment on the banks of the Thames.*

It couldn't have been more blatant — in coded language Annie was saying they were lovers!

Lara was shocked. She knew Dominic would never forgive her for splashing his name in what was sure to be a widely read piece, and would take the whole episode as further proof that she couldn't be trusted!

Just like his first love, he would think she had betrayed his secrets. But she hadn't said any of it, and she didn't understand why Annie had included it. She tried to phone the journalist, but her mobile was switched off, and her office said she wasn't available.

As she replaced the receiver, she noticed her answer phone flashing. She had taken to recording all messages on her landline and her mobile when besieged by reporters, finding it easier to deal with their crassness via an impersonal machine than talking to them directly.

Gingerly she listened to the message, and was relieved to hear India's friendly voice. She was coming to London the next day and intended to pop in at ten o'clock on the offchance that Lara would be there. Listening to the date, Lara realised the message had been left the previous day, which meant India would arrive any minute!

She just had time to plump up the cushions on the sofa before the door bell rang.

It was wonderful to see a friendly face!

India swept into the hall and gave Lara an enormous hug.

'You poor girl!' she exclaimed. 'What a horrible time you must be having!'

Lara burst into tears. She was so tired sometimes she thought she'd have to prop her eyes open with matchsticks just to keep awake. India's fierce hug made her realise how tender her whole body felt. She had struggled on alone for so long that finding someone who supported her was a tremendous relief.

'There, there.' India stroked the blonde head on her shoulder. 'It's all right. I know you thought there was no harm in broadcasting your parentage once Hal was appointed and the two of you had met, it's just a shame you didn't give us some warning of what you were going to do first.'

Lara lifted her head sharply. 'You think I did it!'

'I'm not judging you, but, who else could it have been? Who else knew so much about your life with the Dunstans?'

Lara went over to the table and picked up Malcolm's article. She passed it to India, pointing at the photograph. 'My cousin,' was all she said.

India looked surprised and then relieved.

'Oh! Now I understand!' she said. 'I

was so sure spilling the beans like that went against your character that I just thought it was your relationship with Dominic that made you do it.'

'With Dominic? Why would you think that?'

India gave her a knowing smile. 'We both know how you feel about each other — '

'*Used* to feel about each other — '

'*Still* feel about each other,' she said with a firm glint in her eyes, 'I'm sure this is just a temporary hitch. I thought you wanted to test if he would still love you when there was no longer any reason for him to keep you quiet. Remember you told me you thought he was Hal's minder?'

Lara did remember, and she would give anything to be back at that point now, but the truth was that time had marched on, and Dominic had left her far behind.

India held the newspaper in her hand and tapped her finger on Malcolm's photograph. 'This is wonderful news!'

She beamed. 'We must explain it all to Dominic at once!'

'It won't do any good,' Lara passed over The Meeting Point. 'I was trying to make things right with this,' she said, 'to get Hal off the hook. No one would speak to me, and it was the only thing I could think of, but the writer has put in a lot of stuff I didn't say, stuff about Dominic, and he will never forgive that.'

India quickly scanned the magazine.

'We ordered a copy, but it hadn't arrived by the time I left,' she explained.

It was typical of her, Lara thought, that she hadn't needed to read the article before visiting. Hal and Dominic would have insisted on checking what had been said before risking their reputations.

'Oh, dear!' India scanned the article. 'I see it all now. Annie Kelly — yes, she would want to write about Dom.'

'But why?'

India sighed. 'Has Dominic ever told

you about the first great love of his life?' she asked.

'No, but Henrietta did.'

'So you know he was badly let down by a woman he trusted?'

Lara nodded. 'She married the MD of the rival company, didn't she?'

'Yes, but it didn't last. When he divorced her she tried to win Dominic back, but not surprisingly, he wasn't having any of it. She got bitter and twisted over the whole thing, and the more successful he became, the more bitter and twisted she got.'

'What's that got to do with this article?'

'She'd been a journalist, and went back to it when her husband left her. It probably wasn't a good idea joining The Meeting Point — it must mean that every day she interviews people who are living the life she aspired to and she would now be enjoying with Dom if she'd stayed with him. Her name was Anita Kelly when I knew her, though I see she calls herself Annie these days.'

Lara suddenly felt very sick.

Dominic would never believe she hadn't planned this now, and she knew she had lost him for ever. She rushed to the bathroom and retched over the basin.

'Are you all right?' India looked concerned.

Lara waved her worries aside and quickly rinsed her mouth.

'Why would she do this?' she cried. 'What could she hope to gain?'

'Dominic,' India said shortly. 'She's no fool and would have seen by the way you act that you're hopelessly in love with him.' Lara opened her mouth to protest, but India continued relentlessly. 'Anyone can see that! And for all she knew, he was in love with you too, so she had to make sure it looked as if you had done something he would find beyond the pale.'

'So she's made it look as if I broke his trust.'

'Exactly.'

Lara sat down heavily in the armchair

behind her. 'If you told him the truth, do you think he'd believe you?' she asked, hoping against hope.

India considered. 'The trouble is, Lara, he was talking about the article before it came out, saying it was common knowledge you'd approached the author yourself, and had negotiated a tremendous deal. Obviously Anita again, spreading rumours. I wasn't bothered by what he was saying because I knew that even if it were true, which I doubted, there would be a perfectly reasonable explanation that would win him over. However, I'm afraid when he finds out that Anita wrote the piece, he may well think you simply sold him down the river.'

Lara began to cry, and India took her hand.

'I f-feel so strange and so tired and I don't know what's wrong with me,' she gasped.

'Don't you, Lara? I think I do,' India said gently. 'Tired, over-emotional, being sick . . . ' She left the rest unsaid.

'Oh, my goodness!' Lara's hand flew to her mouth. 'I can't be! I mustn't be!'

Even as she had denied her condition, a thrill of pleasure made Lara's heart beat faster. She was surprised she didn't feel more concerned — she had been programmed to recognise the perils of pre-marriage pregnancy by stern homilies from Mrs Dunstan, but she recognised the difference in their situations.

Mum had been looking at it from the point of view of having to give a baby up for adoption, whereas she had no intention of doing that with Dominic's love child. This baby would be hers, and she would never be parted from it. She would have her own family.

'You'll have to tell Dominic.'

'Never!' That was the one thing she was absolutely sure of. 'If he didn't want me before I was pregnant, I certainly don't want to be acceptable just because I'm carrying his child!'

'Now, Lara — '

'No! With the money I was paid for

the article I have enough to tide me over, but I can't stay here. I need to go somewhere I won't be recognised until after the birth. I suppose I could let this place out . . . ' She was already making plans.

'Well, if you're sure . . . ' India's tone showed she was not. 'My family have a holiday place in the wilds of Norfolk. It's miles from anywhere, and we don't use it much. You could stay there.'

* * *

So it was arranged, and three weeks later Lara was ensconced at Old Thatch, a three bed-roomed cottage deep in the countryside, surrounded by the flat, prairie-like Norfolk fields.

She had bought an old banger to get around in, and kept herself to herself. Only India knew where she had gone. They spoke on the phone regularly but she didn't visit in case the secret should get out.

'Don't you feel lonely?' India was

worried at Lara's isolation.

'No — funnily — I feel completely at peace.'

And she did.

At last she would have her own blood family, a child that was part of Dominic and of her. When she thought of him now, it was with gratitude. She had lost him, but acknowledged she would always love him, and he had given her this matchless gift. It was far more than she ever could have dreamed of.

12

The summer sun beat down relentlessly on the parched East Anglian garden, and Lara placed her daughter Sally back in the large carriage pram, before straightening up to survey the view.

Yesterday the field behind the cottage had been a rustling plain of golden wheat, but the combine harvesters had been running late into the night, and today only stubble remained, with large round stacks set at regular intervals.

Now they were working on the field beyond, and the hum of the machinery was the only sound of man in that blazing afternoon. Soon autumn would be upon them, and they would need to leave their hideaway and return to London, as India's sister was coming home from Singapore and needed somewhere to stay.

Lara would not be sorry to go. She

had loved the freedom of the wide open spaces, but she was a Londoner, and missed the parks and theatres and lights and regular public transport. It wouldn't be a complete goodbye to Norfolk, because India had said when her sister had found somewhere permanent to live, Lara could borrow the cottage in the future and bring Sally down on holiday.

She stretched languidly, and padded back to the picnic rug she had placed under the fronds of the massive weeping willow that dwarfed the back garden. Leaning back against the bole of the tree, she continued with the novel she was reading. But her mind wasn't on it, and her thoughts returned to her daughter — and then, as they so often did, to the man who had given her this precious gift.

She had thought time would ease the pain, that after a while she would dream about him less frequently, ache for him less intensely. But it had not got better; it had got worse.

Some women had only one great love in them, like her own mother, and now she knew she was made that way, too. Sally, mercifully, took up a great deal of her time, but when the baby slept, there was nothing to hide the great gaping emptiness Lara felt inside.

He had sent her a postcard that she received before she moved, obviously in retaliation to her article in The Meeting Point. It was a copy of *Les Amants*. There was no message, and there didn't need to be; the meaning was clear. Hadn't he said that the picture reminded him of the duplicity of the female gender?

Not so much 'love is blind', she thought unhappily as she stared at the hooded faces of the two lovers, *more 'love is treacherous'*.

That he thought so badly of her she found hard to bear. People said it was better to have loved and lost than never to have loved at all, but apart from the fact that if she had not loved she would not have Sally, she didn't agree with the homily.

Before she met Dominic she had been unaware of the overwhelming power of love — the peaks, the pain, the passion — and having experienced them, she hated the thought that they were lost to her for ever. Because she knew if it wasn't Dominic loving her, it would be meaningless.

And he would not be coming back.

She was so thankful to have India as an ally, though even with her she did not share the full extent of her sense of loss, nor the despair she felt on occasion when she imagined her future life alone. India kept her informed of all that was going on in the Lawrence household, and explained their reaction when they read Annie's article . . .

'Hal was very grateful for what you said, and when I explained about your cousin, everyone felt pretty sheepish for thinking you would have been party to the newspaper report. They were all for searching you out to apologise, but I told them you wanted to work things out for yourself, and needed to be given the time to do so.'

'Was Dominic there? Does he know?'

'No, and I didn't think you'd want me to tell him specially. You were so insistent that he shouldn't find out about your condition.'

Lara nodded her agreement. It was best to avoid Dominic. Who knew how he would react?

Her father, now, that was a different matter. It had not taken Hal long to get over his guilt, she thought ruefully. He was apparently making a great success of his new role, and any thought of ousting him had long been forgotten.

He mentioned her quite often when giving interviews, she noticed, speaking as if she were a cherished member of the family and, understanding him as she now did, she knew that he would have convinced himself it was the truth. She had come to accept that he wasn't such a hypocritical man, just a self-indulgent one, and in doing so, recognised that she herself had moved on — away from black and white to seeing the shades in between.

Except in one area. Fidelity was for her a watchword, and the value she would never compromise. Thus far and no further.

India told her that Dominic was spending a lot of his time in Chekurov, and that they hadn't seen him for some time. He felt his work for Hal was done, and now wanted to devote more time to developing Allied Markets in Eastern Europe.

Occasionally his face would appear in a paper, sometimes with a girl in tow. Lara would always wonder whether it was part of her job, or if he had met someone he wanted to be with.

Her eyes grew heavier in the soporific heat, and she gave a great sigh and dozed off, the smell of the wild honeysuckle that clambered through the hedges sweet on the air.

★ ★ ★

So she didn't hear the urgent shrills of the landline, nor the jingles of her mobile that she had left indoors, that went on for quite some time, until India finally admitted Lara must be out, left a message on the mobile, and rang off.

Bother! What was she going to do now? She felt she had broken Lara's confidence, and had wanted at least to warn her. But perhaps it was for the best — Lara couldn't hide all her life, and although she had talked about selling her house and buying one in another part of London, one day it was bound to get out that she'd had a child.

If the truth be known, India could not see that it would matter that much — having a baby out of wedlock was not considered the heinous crime it had been when Lara was born, and if Dominic found out now, he could hardly think Lara was trying to trap him, as to date she had managed very well without him.

Of course, he was about to find out. At first India hadn't known what suddenly made him determined to find Lara, but he had come, storming down to the Hall, and when she had said Hal wasn't there, he'd told her he hadn't come to see Hal, he wanted to talk to her.

'Well, I'm flattered, Dom, of course, though I can't imagine what about.' She thought he had aged since she last saw him; there was more grey hair around his temple, and his face was drawn. Eastern Europe was taking its toll.

'I want you to tell me about Lara.' He had said it quietly, but with a certain tension, and she saw he wasn't going to be fobbed off.

'What do you mean?'

'I've just found out about Anita.' His eyes were hard as he spoke. 'Her blasted magazine approached some friends of mine — the Ostens — wanting to do a feature on the new entrepreneurs of Europe, and they accepted.

'Maria Osten could charm the birds out of the trees, and when she got chatting to the young man who was doing the article, she mentioned she knew Lara. He was a monumental gossip, and only too happy to explain exactly what happened. How it was Anita who spread the malicious rumours about Lara doing it all for money and bidding up the price, and that it was Anita, not Lara, who included all the stuff about me. I sent Lara a pretty nasty message when I thought she had set me up, and I owe it to her to apologise.'

'Well, I'm glad you found out the truth.' India smiled. 'But why have you come to me?'

'Oh, come on, India.' He sounded exasperated. 'She had to have had help to have moved so quickly. I contacted the estate agents who let her house out and through a little judicious flirting — quite harmless I assure you — I got your name as the contact. Anyway, it had to be you. Of all the Lawrences you're the kindest — the only one, actually, who puts others first.'

India turned away and blew her nose vigorously.

'You must know that.' He was gentler now. 'Hal likes to make all these noises about other women and open marriages, but he'd be lost without you. And you're been a real mother to Henrietta, and now, I think, also to Lara.'

India shrugged her shoulders. 'She's a lovely girl, but she wants to be left in peace.'

'I'm not intending to declare war,' he said. 'I don't have any intention of trying to revive things. Yes, I could see at the time you'd sussed our relationship — but that was then and this is now. I simply want to say sorry and move on.'

'I'll tell her.'

'I'm going to tell her myself.'

She had argued, but he had been resolute, and eventually she told him the address, consoling herself that she would be able to phone Lara and prepare her. If she didn't want him to see Sally, she'd have time to make other arrangements.

But she hadn't allowed for the fact that Lara might not pick up, and eventually just had to hope that she'd see the voicemail before Dominic's imminent arrival.

★   ★   ★

The sun was much further across the sky when Lara awoke, but it was still hot, and Sally was crying hungrily. She picked her up and carried her under the tree, where she settled down to feed her. Her tiny eyes, dark as her father's, watched closely, and her little pink hands screwed up into fists of pleasure.

This is heaven — all it needs to be perfect is for Dominic to be here. But as she realised what she'd imagined, she gave herself a shake, disturbing Sally, who gave a wail of temper.

'Shh,' she whispered, leaned back again and closed her eyes. A car pulled up down the lane; the farmer come to see how the combining was going, she expected.

* ★ ★ ★ *

Dominic walked along to the end of the track and saw the cottage nestled among the trees. He rang the doorbell, but no one came, and he slammed his hand against the wall with disappointment. Where was she — and what was he going to say to her when he saw her?

He ran his hand through his hair and decided he would stay until she returned — but not here in the front garden, where there was no let up from the burning sun. There were trees round the back of the house which meant there must be some shade, so he walked down the side of the cottage, hidden by the overgrown privet hedge — and then stopped in his tracks.

She was wearing a soft green dress, sitting under a weeping willow with her legs stretched out in front of her, and her hair hanging around her shoulders covering whatever it was she was holding in her arms. She looked like a wood nymph, pale and pure and —

She sat up, and he felt as if he had been kicked in the stomach as he realised what she was doing. He shouldn't have come — why hadn't India told him? Did she think he deserved this shock for treating Lara the way he had?

He clenched his fists as he imagined the husband and father of the baby, and was about to turn and leave, when he considered the dates . . .

Could it be? Surely she would have told him!

She rocked the child across her shoulder and stood up and walked out into the sunshine towards the pram. She bent to settle the child, and turned — to face Dominic Leigh.

'The child is mine,' he said.

It was not a question.

Lara stood rooted to the spot, her face ashen, her slanting green eyes nervously watching him.

'You don't have to have anything to do with her. I'm not asking for any kind of support.'

A girl, then.

'What you ask for and what you get in life are two very different things. It's not just up to you. Our daughter, as I have just learned she is, has a father as well as a mother!'

He looked down at the child and felt such a wave of paternal pride, such an outpouring of love, that he knew he would have to reach an accommodation with Lara. He had to be involved. How could Hal have borne knowing he had a girl like this somewhere and not sought her out? How could he have given her away?

'What's her name?' he asked, and when he was told, he bent down and whispered, 'Hello, Sally.' His daughter eyed him curiously.

'Why did you come?' Lara asked, trying to drag her eyes away from all the things she loved about him: his granite jaw, his liquid eyes, his long legs.

'I learned the truth about the magazine,' he said shortly. 'I sent you a hurtful card and I wanted to apologise.'

'For not trusting me? It's interesting, isn't it, that whereas I've proved trustworthy, you've shown yourself to be quite untrustworthy?'

She sounded bitter.

'With good reason,' he insisted. 'You did go to the press with the story of your relationship to Hal in the first place.'

'No, I did not!'

'Don't be ridiculous, Lara, how else would they have known all that stuff about your childhood?'

So the Lawrences hadn't told him.

'From my cousin, Malcolm Peters.'

He recognised the name. Since hitting the high spots with his story on Lara, Peter had joined the staff of a salacious Sunday newspaper, and had made a name for himself 'exposing' any number of unfortunates.

He was both ashamed and elated. Ashamed that he had doubted her, and elated that she had not broken his trust.

'Lara, what can I say?'

He moved towards her, but she didn't get a chance to answer, because suddenly he was kissing her, and she had her arms around him and held him close.

'Later,' she said when he broke for air, 'we'll say what has to be said later, but for now you need to get to know your daughter.'

And she picked Sally up from her pram and deposited her in his arms.

He sat on the rug and as Lara watched him struggling with the bottle, she remembered India's words: *Even today it is all too easy for a man to walk away from his offspring.*

Dominic was man enough to stay.

13

The watery late September sun shone through the stained glass window, falling on the burnished reds and golds of the formal flower arrangement near the altar.

Wyscom Church was packed, and as she stood at the threshold on her father's arm, Lara thought how warm and welcoming it looked.

Hal had been horrified at the thought of another registry office wedding, and insisted on hosting the marriage of Lara and Dom at the Hall.

She was wearing a dress of ivory silk, with a long train flowing out behind her, and round her neck she wore the same diamond choker that her mother had worn on her wedding day, a quarter of a century ago.

'You look gorgeous, sis,' Henrietta had exclaimed before setting off from the Hall with little Sally, ahead of the bridal car.

'She's right, you know,' Hal agreed mistily. 'And so like your dear mother.'

Lara patted his arm.

The more she got to know him, the fonder she became of her reprobate of a father, but she had had to accept that he had a selective memory that could render him innocent of any past wrongdoings, and romanticised his involvement in everything.

The hundred-year-old organ struck up the chords of the wedding march, and then she was walking forward, arm in arm with her father, towards her future and her love.

She spied Maria and Paul Osten near the front of the little parish church, and Maria raised her hands above her head and gave Lara the victory wave of a boxer.

I told you so! she mouthed.

The choir broke into her favourite hymn, and as Lara approached the groom, he turned to face her, his expression one of admiration and love.

She felt so happy she had to bite her tongue to stop herself from crying.

As they left the church after the ceremony, Dominic whispered, 'I love you.'

This time it was she who stood with Hal and India at the head of the receiving line at Wyscom Old Hall, and she who sat at the top table, enjoying the speeches and laughter.

'A penny for them,' Dominic said, as he led her round the dance floor.

She admitted she'd been thinking of the Dunstans, the parents who'd brought her up and who would have loved to have seen her settled.

'Their greatest reward would have been to have known you were happy,' he said, 'and I intend to make you very, very happy, my darling girl.'

'You already have,' she said. 'You taught me what love is.'

He gave her the full effect of his dark, hypnotic eyes. 'And you taught me how to trust.'

He buried his head in her flaxen hair and she knew her life was complete.

TWICE IN A LIFETIME

Jo Bartlett

It's been eighteen months since Anna's husband Finn died. Craving space to consider her next steps, she departs the city for the Cornish coast and the isolated Myrtle Cottage. But the best-laid plans often go awry, and when Anna's beloved dog Albie leads her away from solitude and into the path of Elliott, the owner of the nearby adventure centre, their lives become intertwined. As Anna's attraction to Elliott grows, so does her guilt at betraying Finn, until she remembers his favourite piece of advice: you only live once . . .